Rom.
HAN
PB

**ave a feeling you're being**
**too hard on yourself."**

"            rue. I was too caught up with being
a             ved Dana—but my job always came
f            a lot of things suffered because of
t            ch gazed at her, his face somber.
"            e a lot of regrets in my past, Tess."

"All we can do is learn from our mistakes and
move on."

A ghost of a s                                          s
lips. "You sou

She smiled in                                        his
advice?"

"I'm trying."

"Speaking of your uncle, won't you be late…?"

Mitch glanced at his watch. There was no
way he'd make it to his uncle's farm before
dark. But somehow he didn't care. "He'll
understand. Besides, when it comes to regrets,
the past hour spent with you isn't one of
them."

## Books by Irene Hannon

Steeple Hill Love Inspired

*Home for the Holidays #6
*A Groom of Her Own #16
*A Family To Call Her Own #25
It Had To Be You #58
One Special Christmas #77
The Way Home #112
Never Say Goodbye #175
Crossroads #224

*Vows

## IRENE HANNON

has been a writer for as long as she can remember. This prolific author of romance novels for both the inspirational and traditional markets began her career at age ten, when she won a story contest conducted by a national children's magazine. Today, in addition to penning her heartwarming stories of love and faith, Irene keeps quite busy with her day job in corporate communications. In her "spare" time, she enjoys performing in community musical theater productions.

Irene and her husband, Tom—whom she describes as "my own romantic hero"—make their home in St. Louis, Missouri.

# CROSSROADS

## IRENE HANNON

*Love Inspired*

Published by Steeple Hill Books

STEEPLE HILL BOOKS

Steeple
Hill®

ISBN 0-373-87231-3

CROSSROADS

Visit us at www.steeplehill.com

**Printed in U.S.A.**

You changed my mourning into dancing; you
took off my sackcloth and clothed me with gladness.
—*Psalms* 30:11

To my precious niece, Catherine Moira,
who has been such a blessing in our lives.
May all your tomorrows be filled with joy and love.

# *Chapter One*

Bruce Lockwood banged the door and stormed into the kitchen, his eyes flashing. "Mr. Jackson is a—"

"Bruce!" Tess gave her fourteen-year-old son a stern warning look. She knew exactly what he was about to say, and she didn't allow that kind of language in the house.

"—creep!" Bruce finished more tamely, slamming his books onto the table.

Tess cringed. She hadn't exactly had the best day herself, and she wasn't sure she was up to another tirade about Southfield High's principal. She took a deep breath, willing the dull ache in her temples to subside.

"Do you want to tell me what happened?"

Bruce gave her a sullen look. "He's just a creep, that's all." The boy withdrew a card from his pocket and tossed it onto the table. "He wants you to call and make an appointment with him."

Tess frowned and reached for the card, her stomach

clenching. The adjustment from small-town school in Jefferson City, Missouri, to big-city school in St. Louis had been difficult for him, particularly midyear. If there had been any way to delay their move until the end of the term, she would have. But the unexpected merger of her newspaper with a larger chain had left her a victim of downsizing, and the offer from a community newspaper in suburban St. Louis had seemed the answer to a prayer. She'd been able to find a comfortable apartment near the office in a quiet suburb, and had hoped that the small-town feel of the area would ease the transition to their new environment. It had worked for her, but not for Bruce.

Tess glanced down at the card. "Mitch Jackson, principal." Her frown deepened. Parents weren't usually contacted unless there was a good reason. The ache in her temples began to throb, and she looked over at her son. He was watching her—his body posture defiant, but his eyes wary.

"Why does he want to meet with me?"

"I didn't do anything wrong," Bruce countered.

Tess folded her arms across her chest, her lips tightening into a thin line. "I didn't say you did. I just asked why he wants to see me," she replied, struggling to keep her temper in check.

"Because he's a creep!"

"That's not an answer."

"It's true! Ever since I transferred to that dumb school he's been watching me, just waiting for me to mess up. He should still be a cop, the way he's on me for every little thing."

Tess held the card up. "What 'little thing' prompted this?"

Bruce glared at her. "You're as bad as he is. Always asking questions, always breathing down my neck. Why can't people just leave me alone?"

Tess stared at her son. How had her relationship with Bruce deteriorated in two short months? There was a time when they used to talk, when he shared things with her. But since coming to St. Louis he'd withdrawn, shutting her out of his life and his thoughts. She'd tried to draw him out, but the demands of her new job had left her too little time to spend with her son during this critical transition period. Whatever his problems at school, she knew she shared the blame. Slowly she sat down on the kitchen chair, drew a steadying breath and looked up at him.

"Maybe because people care."

Bruce gave a dismissive snort. "Mr. Jackson doesn't care. He's just nosy."

"I care."

He was disarmed by her quiet tone and steady gaze, and his expression softened briefly. But a moment later the defiant mask slipped back into place. "You're too busy to care."

His words cut deeply, and Tess's stomach again contracted painfully. "That's not true, Bruce. You always come first in my heart. But I have to put in a little extra time at the beginning to learn the ropes. You know I need this job."

He shoved his fists into the pockets of baggy slacks that hung on his too-thin hips. "Yeah. Thanks to…Dad." His tone was bitter, the last word sarcastic. He turned away and stared out the window, his shoulders stiff with tension. "I wish we still lived in Jeff City," he said fiercely.

Another painful tug on the heartstrings. "I do, too. But this was the best offer I had. I'm still here for you, though. You know that, Bruce. I may be your mom, but I'm also your friend."

He shrugged. "I have other friends."

*And you aren't one of them.* The message was clear. And it hurt, even though she was glad that he'd finally connected with a group at the school, where cliques were already well established. But she was also a bit uneasy. He never talked about his friends, never brought them home, never even introduced her to any of them. "I'd like to meet them," she replied.

"They're *my* friends, Mom," he said tersely, turning back to her. "Do I have to share everything?"

She looked at the gangly teenager across from her and wondered not for the first time where her sweet young son had gone. She missed the endearingly protective little boy with the touching sensitivity and wise-beyond-his-years perceptiveness. She'd always known Bruce would grow up. She'd just never expected him to grow *away,* she realized, her eyes misting.

When Bruce spoke again, his voice was gentler. Maybe the sensitivity wasn't gone entirely, Tess thought hopefully.

"I'm okay, Mom. Really. You don't have to worry about me."

Tess fished in the pocket of her slacks for a tissue. "Worrying is part of the job description for motherhood," she replied, dabbing at her eyes. "Look, Bruce, I need to know what Mr. Jackson wants to talk to me about. I don't want to be blindsided. You've been avoiding the question, and I need an answer."

He shrugged dismissively. ''It was nothing to get excited about. Some of the guys had been smoking in an empty classroom, and Mr. Jackson showed up. He could smell the smoke, and he said he was going to put us on report and talk to our parents.''

Tess stared at Bruce. ''You were smoking?''

He looked at her in disgust and reached for his books. ''See? Even *you* jump to conclusions. I said *some* of the guys were smoking. Not *me*. Why does everybody always think the worst?''

Tess watched with a troubled expression as he strode down the hall and disappeared into his room. She'd heard that many adolescents developed an attitude, but somehow she'd never expected it of Bruce.

Wearily she rose and set the kettle on the stove. A soothing cup of tea would help, she decided, though what she really needed was someone with whom she could share her concerns and frustrations about single parenthood and adolescent boys. She'd tried prayer, which usually anchored her. But this time her prayers hadn't had their usual calming effect. She still felt unsteady—and unsure. About a lot of things. Was Bruce's behavior normal for his age—or was it indicative of more serious problems? Did all teenage boys get involved in minor infractions as they tested their wings? Did they all shut out their parents? Would it help if he had a father figure?

Tess poured the water into a mug and carried it back to the table, propping her chin in her hand as she absently dunked the tea bag. That last question had popped up over and over again during the past six years, and always she came to the same conclusion. Yes, it would help if he had a father figure. But only if it was a *good* father figure. And her ex-husband, Peter, certainly hadn't been it. Not by a long shot. She'd stayed with him far too long as it was. Might still be there if she hadn't found…

Impatiently Tess dismissed that line of thought. Peter was history. He'd done so much damage to his son's self-esteem that Tess still spent sleepless nights wondering if it could ever be truly undone. As for her own self-esteem…he'd done a number on that, too. At least she'd been older and, with her strong faith, better equipped to deal with it. She was a survivor. Even so, years later, the scars remained with her, as well. Peter had destroyed her confidence, leaving her unsure of her intelligence, of her talents…of herself as a woman. The only things she *had* been sure about were her mothering skills.

Tess's gaze fell on the principal's card, and slowly she picked it up, her spirits nose-diving.

She *had* been sure. Until now.

"Have a seat. Mr. Jackson is just finishing up another meeting. He'll be with you in a moment."

Tess nodded at the receptionist in the small ante-room outside the principal's office and headed toward a chair in the far corner. As she sat, she took a deep breath and nervously hitched her shoulder bag into a more secure position. Thanks to her son, she'd received the dreaded summons of her childhood. She'd been called to the principal's office.

Memories came flooding back of stern-faced Mr. Markham, whose very presence had intimidated even the most self-assured students, let alone someone like bookish, shy Tess. She'd lived in fear of committing some transgression that would call her to his attention and result in a humiliating penalty. Strange how those childhood fears could sweep back so compellingly. In a way, she felt as if she was ten years old again. And she didn't like it.

Suddenly the door to the inner office opened, and Tess's heart began to hammer painfully in her chest. She took another deep breath as her fingers clenched around the strap of her shoulder bag. *This is ridiculous,* she admonished herself. *You're an adult. He can't do anything to you. Calm down!*

A bored-looking woman in a suit that Tess figured cost more than she made in a month crossed the threshold, followed by a slightly balding man. He glanced impatiently at his watch, then turned back to speak to someone just out of sight inside the doorway.

"We'll consider your suggestion," he said coldly.

"I told you all along that a private school would be better for Jerome. I never did think he'd do well in a…public…environment," the woman said with undisguised disdain.

She swept out without a backward glance, followed by the balding man.

The receptionist watched them leave, then glanced at Tess. Her raised eyebrows and the slight shake of her head spoke more eloquently than words.

"I take it sometimes the parents are worse than the kids," Tess commiserated with a rueful smile, hoping some levity might quell the butterflies in her stomach.

The woman rolled her eyes and rose. "That's putting it mildly. I'll tell Mr. Jackson you're here."

The woman stepped up to his door, knocked softly,

then entered. As she disappeared inside and closed the door, Tess took a deep breath and braced herself.

Inside the office, the receptionist regarded the tall, broad-shouldered man who stood gazing out the window. "Tess Lockwood is here, Mitch," she said. "Think you can handle one more parent today?"

Mitch turned, and the late-afternoon sun high-lighted the glints of auburn in his dark hair. "That depends on her mood," he said with a sigh.

The woman tilted her head consideringly. "I'd say she's nervous. Maybe even a little scared. Actually, she doesn't look much older than some of your students. My guess is she was one of those good kids who always went out of her way to avoid being called to the principal's office, and is none too happy—or comfortable—about finding herself in one at this stage in her life."

One corner of Mitch's mouth twitched up. "You missed your calling, you know that? You should have been either a psychologist or a psychic."

She grinned. "No ring, either. And she's alone. Single-parent household."

"Or a detective."

"I'll remind you of those many career options next time I ask for a raise. So should I send her in?"

Mitch hesitated. "Give me five minutes, okay? I want to make a few notes about that last meeting—or should I say confrontation?" he added with a grimace.

"That bad, huh?"

He reached up and massaged the back of his neck. "Karen, let me ask you something. Was I too hard on the King boy?"

She gave an unladylike snort. "I don't think you were hard enough. I would have expelled him."

Mitch smiled. "Thanks for the reality check."

"You're welcome." Karen tilted her head and studied him for a moment. "You look tired."

"Goes with the territory."

"Nope. Don't buy it. You push yourself way too hard. You worry about these kids like they were your own. That's way above and beyond the job description for principals."

He shrugged. "Somebody has to worry about them. And parents don't always do the best job."

Karen shook her head. "I admire your commitment. The world could use more principals like you. Only do me a favor, okay? Try not to take their problems home—at least not every night. You need a life, too."

"I have a life."

"Right," she said dryly. "You spend your days— and a lot of nights—here, then help your uncle on his farm every weekend. Some life."

"It works for me."

She rolled her eyes. "You're a lost cause, Mitch Jackson."

As she closed the door behind her, Mitch shoved his hands into his pockets and turned back to the window, his gaze troubled. Karen was right. He didn't have much of a life. And he wasn't sure his sacrifice was making much difference. Since switching careers from law enforcement to education, he'd run into far too many parents like those who had just exited his office. Overprotective. Unwilling to admit their offspring might be wrong. Blaming the system for their child's problems.

There were good parents, too. But in his job he saw mostly the ones who really didn't care. Or who were too busy to pay much attention to what their kids did. Or who were so absorbed in their own lives or careers that their priorities were screwed up. Or who abdicated their parental duties by treating their teenagers like adults instead of like the kids they were—desperate for guidance despite their facade of confidence and bravado. They were the same type of parents he'd run into as a cop. Only in his previous career, he'd usually run into them when it was too late—because that's when the law generally got involved. He knew that firsthand—not only as a cop, but as a parent.

The sudden, familiar clench in his gut made him suck in his breath, and his hands knotted into fists as memories came flooding back. Nightmare memories that haunted his dreams and far too often jolted him like an electric shock during his waking hours. He closed his eyes as the pain washed over him. *Dear God, will it never go away?* he cried in silent anguish. The searing pain was as fresh as it had been six years before. A pain so intense it had motivated him to switch careers. Had driven him to try to catch kids' problems at an early stage, before it was too late. Had compelled him to transform the job of principal from deskbound administrator to one of hands-on involvement and intervention. His atypical methods had raised more than a few eyebrows. But they were often effective. And those successes were what made his job worthwhile, what gave his life meaning.

A discreet knock on the door interrupted his thoughts, and he glanced toward it as Karen stuck her head in.

"Ready?"

No, he wasn't. But he couldn't put if off any longer. After the meeting with Jerome's parents, Mitch wasn't optimistic about that boy's future. But maybe Bruce had a better support system. That was one of the big differences between his job and his personal life, he reflected as he drew a deep breath. There was always another chance with his job.

"Yes. Send her in."

As Karen ushered in Tess Lockwood, Mitch did a rapid assessment. His secretary had been right about the woman's appearance. Though she had to be in her mid-thirties, she could easily pass for a college student. Her boxy pantsuit couldn't quite hide her slender curves, nor could the staid barrette at her nape successfully restrain her shoulder-length russet hair. A few tendrils softly framed her face, which would be lovely if it wasn't so tense. But even the strain in her eyes couldn't take away from their vivid green depths, framed by a thick fringe of lashes.

Karen also seemed to be on target about Ms. Lockwood's attitude. She obviously didn't want to be here, and she was clearly nervous. But why? Was it due to legitimate worry about her son, inconvenience to herself or anger at a system that she believed was the real cause of the problem, as Jerome's parents did?

Mitch didn't know, but he'd find out soon enough. And in the meantime, some subtle nuance that he couldn't put his finger on told him to handle this woman with kid gloves. Maybe it was the fine lines of fatigue around her eyes. Or the death grip she had on her purse strap. Or the caution in her eyes, which seemed to speak of past hurts that had left her unwilling to trust. He had no idea why the warning bell had gone off in his mind. But his instincts had saved his life on more than one occasion when he was a cop, and he wasn't about to question them now.

He smiled and stepped forward, extending his hand. "Ms. Lockwood? I'm Mitch Jackson. It's a pleasure to meet you."

Tess placed her cold fingers in his firm, warm clasp, and for a moment she simply stared at the tall man in front of her. *This* was Bruce's ogre? she thought incredulously. This dark-haired man with the compassionate, deep brown eyes and cordial manner, whose face reflected character and humor and intelligence? *This* was the hated principal? She'd prepared herself for another Mr. Markham, someone pinched-faced with beady eyes and an intimidating demeanor who, with a single look, could make her feel nervous and incompetent as a parent. She had *not* been expecting a handsome contemporary with kind eyes and the rugged physique of an athlete, who radiated virility—and who suddenly made her feel nervous and incompetent on a very different level.

Tess realized that he was waiting for her to reply, and somehow she found her voice. "Th-thank you. Please excuse me for staring," she stammered. "It's just that you aren't exactly…that is, I had a different image of…well, from what Bruce said…" She felt hot color steal onto her cheeks. So much for eloquence and poise. She sounded like an idiot!

But if the man across from her thought so, he was

gallant enough not to show it. Instead, a smile twinkled in his eyes as he gestured toward a seating area next to his desk. "Let me guess. From what Bruce said, you expected a monster with eyes in the back of his head, a fire-breathing dragon intent on burning anyone who comes close, an evil version of a Superman/Santa Claus with X-ray vision and a checklist of bad deeds—or all of the above."

That description pretty much fit her image of Mr. Markham, for whom nothing less than absolute compliance and perfection had sufficed. Thank heaven Mitch Jackson seemed to be cut from different cloth, Tess thought with relief as she sat in one of the upholstered chairs. For one thing, he didn't appear to take himself too seriously. For another, he seemed warm and personable.

"You just described the principal at my grade school," she confessed with a smile.

For a moment Mitch was stunned by the transforming effect of her smile. She looked even younger now, her features relaxing as they softened. Though she wore almost no makeup, her face had a natural loveliness and a certain intriguing—and appealing—wistful quality. Her eyes radiated warmth and intelligence, and for just a moment he found himself drowning in their depths. It was an unexpected—and disconcerting—experience. So he forced himself to focus on the shadows beneath those amazing eyes instead. Shadows that didn't appear to be the result of one sleepless night, but spoke more of long-term strain, stress, overwork—or all three. For some reason, those shadows bothered him more than they should. Which was odd. And way off the subject, he reminded himself.

"I think we all have a principal like that some-where in our memory bank," Mitch commiserated, struggling to regain his balance.

He had an engaging dimple in his left cheek when he smiled, Tess noted distractedly, trying to focus in-stead on the conversation. "Though they probably weren't quite as bad as we remember," she admitted.

"Maybe not. But I'm certainly not the most pop-ular man on campus with some of *my* students. Bruce happens to be one of them."

"Why not?" She hadn't meant to be quite that di-rect, but this man was easy to talk to, and the words were out before she could stop them. Fortunately Mitch didn't seem to mind.

"For a lot of reasons. Number one, I enforce the rules. Number two, I care about my students, and I make it a point to keep my eye on the ones who seem to need a bit of extra supervision. Number three, I used to be a cop, and I can spot trouble—and the potential for trouble—pretty quickly. That's why I've been watching Bruce. He seems to be a basically good kid who just needs a little more help than most to stay on the straight and narrow."

Tess stiffened at what she perceived to be criticism. "You make it sound like he's on the verge of becom-ing a delinquent. Don't you think you're overreacting to one little smoking incident? Which Bruce tells me he didn't even participate in, by the way. Most kids experiment with cigarettes at some point or other. I don't approve, but I don't think it's necessarily a sign of serious trouble."

Mitch frowned. "Is that what he told you? That

this meeting is just about a simple smoking incident?"

Now it was Tess's turn to frown. "Isn't it?"

Mitch rose to retrieve a folder from his desk. As he rejoined her, he flipped it open. "The smoking situation was only the latest in a series of incidents," he informed her, the seriousness of his tone and demeanor in sharp contrast to his initial conversational manner. "Though even that was more than you've been led to believe. Those guys weren't smoking cigarettes. They were smoking a joint."

Tess stared at him incredulously. "You mean marijuana?"

He nodded. "Yes. There was no sign of it when I showed up. But the odor is unmistakable—and lingering."

"Marijuana?" Tess repeated the word in shock. "Drugs? You mean Bruce is involved with drugs?" Now there was a note of panic in her voice, and her fingers tightened convulsively on her purse.

Mitch wished he could bring back her smile of moments before, erase the twin furrows of worry on her brow and ease the tension that had made her skin go taut over the fine bone structure of her face. But his job wasn't to make parents feel good, he reminded himself. It was to help kids.

"I don't think he's into drugs," he replied carefully. "At least not yet. But he hangs around with a rough, older crowd, and sooner or later they'll pull him down to their level. Kids like Bruce are easy prey, Ms. Lockwood. He doesn't seem to have a lot of self-confidence, and it's tough to break into established cliques, especially midyear. That makes him vulnerable to groups that are on the fringe. They offer a haven of friendship that can be very powerful—someone to sit with in the cafeteria, a sympathetic ear, somewhere to belong. A 'home,' if you will.''

"Bruce has a home," Tess protested, a tremor of fear running through her voice.

Mitch studied her for a moment. He knew he was venturing onto shaky ground, but the more information he had, the more likely he could help. "May I ask a question?"

Tess eyed him cautiously. "What is it?"

"Is there a father figure in Bruce's life?"

Tess's eyes went cold. "No."

"Any friends outside of school?"

She swallowed and shook her head. "Not that I know of. It's…hard for him to make friends. His self-esteem isn't…isn't all that high."

"Why not?"

She took a deep breath, and her eyes shuttered. "That's a long story, Mr. Jackson."

"And not a pleasant one, I take it."

"No."

The answer was terse—and telling. For a long moment there was silence, and then Tess spoke again.

"Look, Mr. Jackson, I do the best I can. I'm a single mom who has to work full-time to keep a roof over our heads and food on the table. I try my best to be mother, father and friend. Lately Bruce has been shutting me out. He obviously didn't tell me the whole truth about the smoking incident." She paused and took a deep breath, bracing herself. "You said there were others?"

Mitch nodded and consulted his file. "We haven't

caught the perpetrators, though we have strong suspicions. And in all cases I suspect that Bruce was involved, either as a participant or bystander. Five weeks ago we found obscene graffiti on the wall in one of the boys' rest rooms. The next week several cars in the parking lot were vandalized during a basketball game—tires slashed, rearview mirrors ripped off, long scratches on the sides. Two weeks ago some software disappeared from the computer lab. The smoking incident is the latest problem.''

Tess began to feel ill. ''But you said you have no proof that Bruce was involved in those other things,'' she pointed out faintly, a touch of desperation in her voice. ''Why do you think he is?''

''Because of the group he hangs out with. I won't go so far as to call it a gang, but it's borderline.''

The principal had just confirmed the suspicion that had been niggling at the edge of Tess's consciousness for the past few weeks, and her spirits slipped another notch—as did her confidence. She was trying so hard to juggle the demands and responsibilities of her life. But clearly her best simply wasn't good enough. She was failing Bruce, the only person in the world who mattered to her. And she didn't know what to do about it.

Mitch watched the play of emotions on the face of the woman across from him. Pain. Despair. Panic. On one hand, he hated to put her through this. On the other hand, he felt a sense of relief. The presence of those emotions told him that she cared—truly cared—about her son. She might not know how to help him, but she wanted to—and that was the key. He could work with parents like Tess Lockwood. Because they were generally willing to work with him.

"I'm sorry to upset you, Ms. Lockwood. But it's better to find out now rather than later. And we can work this out, I'm sure."

At the man's gentle tone, Tess's gaze flew to his. She'd expected to be read the riot act from a stern disciplinarian with a shape-up-or-ship-out stance. She *hadn't* expected warmth, caring and the offer of assistance.

Tess's throat tightened and her eyes filmed over with moisture at this stranger's unexpected compassion. She glanced away on the pretense of adjusting the shoulder strap on her purse, willing herself not to cry. She blinked several times, fighting for control, and when she at last looked up, her voice was steady, her gaze direct.

"I agree that sooner is better. I just hope we're soon enough. Bruce is a good boy at heart, Mr. Jackson. And I've tried to be a good parent. But I can see now that I need help. Obviously, parenting isn't one of my talents, and I'd appreciate any advice you can offer."

Mitch caught the glimmer of unshed tears, clearly held in check by the slimmest of control, and frowned. His gut told him that she really was trying her best. But she was clearly stressed to the limit. "I didn't mean to imply that you aren't a good parent, Ms. Lockwood. On the contrary. I can see you care deeply about your son's welfare."

"But that's not enough."

The despair in her voice went straight to his heart, and he had a sudden, unexpected impulse to reach out and take her hand, to reassure her that she wasn't quite as alone as she seemed to feel. But that kind of gesture would be completely inappropriate, he reminded himself sharply. So before he could act on it and embarrass them both, he rose abruptly and walked over to his desk.

The flyer he wanted was right on top, but he made a pretense of shuffling through some papers, buying a moment to compose himself. For some reason, this woman had touched a place deep in his core, nudged feelings that had long lain dormant. He wanted to help her, and not just because it was his job. Which was crazy. After all, he'd just met her. Besides, he wasn't in the market for personal involvements of any kind—especially with mothers of troubled students. And he'd better remember that.

The expression on her face when he turned back almost did him in. Clearly, his abrupt movement had disconcerted her. She looked vulnerable and uncertain and in desperate need of comforting. It took every ounce of his willpower to calmly walk back to his chair and simply hand her the flyer he'd retrieved.

"Caring is the most important thing, Ms. Lockwood," he said, his voice a shade deeper than usual. "But sometimes it does take even more. You might want to attend this meeting next week. Chris Stevens, one of our counselors, is going to talk about the pressures teens face and how parents can help. There'll also be an opportunity for discussion and questions. I think you'll find it worthwhile."

Tess glanced down at the sheet of paper. It had been a long time since anyone had offered a helping hand, and once more her throat constricted with emotion.

"Thank you. I'll do my best to make it." She folded the paper and put it in her purse, then rose. Mitch was instantly on his feet, and when he extended his hand, she once more found her fingers enveloped in his warm grasp.

"In the meantime, I'll keep my eye on Bruce. And don't hesitate to call if you have any other concerns."

Tess gazed up into his kind eyes, and for the briefest moment allowed herself to wonder what life would have been like if Bruce had had a father figure like Mitch Jackson in his life these past few years. Somehow, in her heart, she knew that things would have been a lot different. For him—and for her.

Suddenly afraid that he would read her thoughts, she withdrew her hand and lowered her gaze. "I appreciate your interest," she said, her voice quavering slightly as he walked her to the door.

"It goes with the territory. Goodbye, Ms. Lockwood. And try not to worry. I have a feeling that things are going to improve."

She gazed at him directly then, and once more something in her eyes reached to his very soul. "I hope so, Mr. Jackson. And thank you for caring."

Mitch watched her speculatively as she walked across the reception area and disappeared out the door. Unlike the parents from his previous conference, Tess Lockwood seemed to have taken his comments to heart. He had a feeling that she wouldn't easily dismiss their encounter.

And for reasons that had nothing at all to do with her son, Mitch didn't think he would, either.

# Chapter Two

"Okay, let's talk."

At Tess's no-nonsense tone, Bruce looked up from his desk, his eyes wary. "About what?"

She moved to the side of his bed and sat down. "Guess."

"I suppose Mr. Jackson told you a lot of garbage."

"'Garbage' is a good word for the behavior he discussed."

"I haven't done anything wrong," Bruce declared defensively.

"You know what? I believe you. But from what I heard, you're heading in the wrong direction."

"Mr. Jackson just wants to get me in trouble."

"Wrong. He wants to *keep* you from getting in trouble."

Bruce looked at her defiantly. "So now you're on his side."

"That's right. Because he happens to be on *your* side."

"That's a bunch of—"

"Bruce!"

He clamped his mouth shut and stared at her sullenly.

"That's exactly the kind of behavior I'm talking about. Since when did you start using language like that?"

"Like what?"

"Come off it, Bruce. You've let enough slip these last few weeks for me to realize that you've expanded your vocabulary. And I don't like it."

"Words don't hurt anything."

"I disagree. They hurt your character. And they can also give you a juvenile record if you scratch them on the walls in the boys' rest room."

Bruce's face grew red. "I didn't have anything to do with that."

"I didn't say you did. And I don't believe you vandalized the cars or stole the computer equipment."

"I wasn't smoking, either."

"Maybe not. But when it comes to drugs, the cops bust you first and ask questions later."

He looked at her in confusion. "What are you talking about?"

"Mr. Jackson gave me a few more details about the smoking incident."

He still looked confused. "What does that have to do with drugs?"

Tess stared at him, and slowly the light began to dawn. He honestly didn't know! Relief coursed through her and the tension coiled deep inside eased ever so slightly. "That wasn't just a cigarette, Bruce," she said gently. "It was a joint. Marijuana."

His face blanched. "Who told you that?"

"Mr. Jackson."

"I don't believe it! Besides, how does he know? He didn't see anything."

"He was a cop, remember? He could tell from the smell. You're lucky he contacted *me* instead of the police."

Bruce frowned. "He didn't have a case, anyway," he said slowly, some of his cockiness returning. "There wasn't any evidence. And the smell would have been gone by the time the police got there."

Anger flashed in Tess's eyes. "Maybe the next time you won't be so lucky."

Bruce glared at her defiantly. "I can take care of myself."

"Really? So what are you going to do when they pass around the next joint?"

His gaze skittered away. "I don't have to smoke. They'll be my friends even if I don't."

"They're not your friends *now,* Bruce. They're bad news, and they're going to drag you down with them. Can't you see that?" she pleaded, a note of desperation creeping into her voice.

"No! I like them! They're nice to me! They're the only ones who *are* at that dumb school. Do you know what it's like not to have anyone to sit with at lunch? It su…it stinks! I sat by myself every day until they invited me. I owe them," he said fiercely.

An ominous chill went down Tess's spine. The scenario Bruce had just described was exactly the one Mitch Jackson had used as an example. By drawing him in, by accepting him, the group he'd hooked up with had evoked not only a sense of gratitude, but of obligation. Which could be very dangerous.

"You don't owe them a thing," Tess shot back, but she could see that her words fell on deaf ears. She rose, trying to control her panic. "Okay. Until further notice, you're to come home right after school."

Bruce sent her a venomous look. "You're grounding me?"

"You got it."

"Why? I haven't done anything wrong. You said you believed me."

"I do. But I think you're on dangerous ground."

"So you're going to lock me up? I bet that was Mr. Jackson's idea," he said angrily.

"As a matter of fact, it wasn't. I thought it up all by myself."

"I'll still see the guys at school," he countered defiantly.

"That's true. But I think Mr. Jackson will be keeping his eye out for you there."

"I should have figured you two would team up," he said bitterly. "Adults always stick together."

Instead of responding, Tess simply left the room. Once out of sight, she leaned against the wall, struggling to control the tremors that ran through her body. *Please, Lord, help me!* she prayed desperately as another wave of panic washed over her. She had no idea how to deal with this situation. But she knew she needed help. The counseling session Mitch had invited her to couldn't come soon enough. Because Bruce was in way over his head.

And so was she.

\* \* \*

"Morning, Tess. Have I got a story for you!"

Tess glanced up at the managing editor and smiled. Caroline James was about the same age as Tess, but she was light years ahead of the paper's newest reporter in terms of sophistication and polish. Why someone with Caroline's experience, abilities and contacts was content to be the managing editor of a suburban newspaper was beyond Tess's understanding. She was just grateful to have the chance to hone her skills under the guidance of a true pro.

"Hi, Caroline. What's up?"

"A great coup for our little paper, that's what." Caroline sat on the single chair in Tess's cube and crossed her legs, revealing their shapely length under her fashionably short skirt. As she leaned back, her silk blouse shimmered in the overhead light, as did her simple but classic gold necklace. Style. Class. Poise. Caroline had it all, Tess thought wistfully. In her tailored slacks and baggy sweater, Tess felt dowdy and plain by comparison. Not to mention awkward. Even on her best days, Tess didn't move with the lithe grace that came so naturally to Caroline. Yet her boss was completely down-to-earth, without a pretentious bone in her body, and she had gone out of her way to make Tess feel at home on the paper. It was hard to be envious of someone so nice.

"Sounds promising," Tess replied.

"More than promising. A sure thing. It seems we have a man of great distinction right here in our midst."

"Really? Who?"

"One Mitch Jackson, local principal."

Tess stared at Caroline in shock. "Mitch Jackson?"

"Yeah." Caroline tilted her head and gazed at Tess. "You look funny. Do you know him?"

Tess nodded and cleared her throat. "Yes. Sort of. That is, we've met. Briefly. He's the principal at my son's school."

"Great! A connection! That will make it even easier to scoop the daily. Hopefully he'll give us first crack."

"At what?"

"A feature profile. He's just been chosen to receive the governor's award for excellence in education. He's introduced some really innovative programs at the school. We've tried to do a story on him before, but apparently he prefers to stay out of the limelight."

Tess tried to calm the sudden pounding of her heart. "So what makes you think he'll be any different this time?"

"The school board," Caroline informed Tess smugly. "My sources tell me they've been after him for quite a while to be more forthcoming with the press about his programs. Good publicity for the school district, which is handy when it comes time for funding. They aren't going to let him get away with a 'no comment' this time, I guarantee it. Besides, if you know him, we already have an in."

"I don't really know him, Caroline. We only met once."

"That's okay. He'll remember you."

Tess frowned. "Why do you say that?"

"Because you are one attractive gal. You have terrific eyes, gorgeous hair, a great figure—even if you do hide it under oversize clothes—and you're single. What guy wouldn't notice?''

Tess felt hot color creep onto her cheeks. ''I think maybe you need to get your contacts changed,'' she said with an embarrassed smile.

''Trust me on this,'' Carolyn said with a grin. ''By the way, I understand he's single. Not to mention handsome, if you can believe this picture that just came over the wire.'' She tossed a clipping onto Tess's desk. ''Probably make a great catch.''

''Maybe *you* should interview him,'' Tess suggested. ''I'm not in the market.''

A shadow passed over Caroline's eyes, so brief Tess almost missed it. ''Me, neither. I already had my taste of heaven,'' she said lightly, but Tess heard the whisper of sadness in her voice. ''Anyway, personal stuff aside, you're one of our best feature writers. You'll be able to do this story justice. What do you say?''

Tess frowned. She hadn't counted on another opportunity to spend time one-on-one with Southfield High's principal. In fact, she was still recovering from their last encounter. She'd lain awake far too many nights thinking about Mitch Jackson. And that was based purely on a meeting that had focused on *Bruce*. Now she was being asked to get ''up close and personal'' with *him* for a profile. The mere thought of it sent a delicious, anticipatory tingle down her spine. Which was silly, of course. She would be dealing with him in a purely professional capacity, much as he'd dealt with her the last time.

Yet the yearning to see him again was inexplicably strong. For some reason, just being in his presence

made her feel…*tingly* was the word that came to
mind. For the first time in years she'd felt more like
a desirable woman than a mom. And it was renewing,
quenching a place in her heart that had long been
parched and lifeless. Though she wasn't in the market
for romance, she was enough of a romantic to want
to have that feeling again, if only for the duration of
one more meeting.

"Don't think so hard, Tess," Caroline advised her
with an understanding smile. "I can see you're interested in the story—and maybe in the man. Just go for
it." Before Tess could reply, Caroline stood and made
her way to the door, pausing on the threshold. "In
case I haven't told you lately, we're really glad to
have you aboard here. Not only are you an excellent
writer, you're smart and intuitive, and you have a
warmth that makes people open up. We're lucky to
have someone with your talent. So give this a shot,
okay?"

Tess watched Caroline walk away, then slowly
reached for the clipping and studied the grainy picture
of Mitch Jackson. Her boss was right—he was one
handsome man. But he was also much more. She had
seen and felt firsthand things that the picture didn't
reveal. The caring and compassion in his insightful
eyes. His ability to make you feel that *your* problems
were *his* problems. The innate strength and sense of
honor that seemed to radiate from his very core. His
total dedication and commitment to his students.
None of those things could be captured by a picture.

Nor could his almost tangible virility. It awakened
yearnings in her that had long lain dormant, yearnings
she thought had slowly withered up and blown away

like a once-beautiful autumn leaf. It was frightening—and intimidating—to discover that those yearnings could so unexpectedly be brought back to life. Not that it mattered, of course. Despite what Caroline had said, someone like Mitch Jackson would never give her a second look. Even if she wanted him to. Which she didn't, she told herself firmly. The last thing she needed in her already complicated life was another complication. Or distraction. And she knew instinctively that Southfield High's principal could definitely be both.

Tess deliberately shifted her attention to the sketchy text that accompanied the photo. There wasn't much in it that she didn't already know. He'd been a cop earlier in his career, had moved to St. Louis two years ago, was a hands-on principal who believed in getting involved in the lives of his students. The only new piece of information she gleaned from the write-up was that prior to coming to St. Louis he'd lived in Chicago.

Tess's face grew thoughtful. Clearly there was a whole lot more to Mitch's story. Whether or not he'd reveal it, however, remained to be seen. But she did seem to have a knack for getting people to open up and reveal more about themselves than they'd planned to. And she liked challenges, especially intriguing ones.

Tess glanced back at Mitch's picture. *Intriguing* was a good word for Southfield High's principal. Other words came to mind as well, but she chose to ignore them. She didn't have the time or inclination for romance, she reminded herself. What she did have was a son to raise—a job that required her full-time attention. And she would do well to remember that.

Tess glanced around the crowded meeting room, relieved to see that other parents also seemed to feel the need for more information about raising teenagers. It helped a bit to know that she wasn't alone.

Her quick scan revealed few available seats, but she spotted one in the middle of the last row and quickly made her way toward it. As she carefully edged past those already seated, trying not to step on toes as she went, she glanced at her watch. She'd made it with two minutes to spare.

Tess was still settling in when a familiar voice over the microphone drew her startled gaze. She hadn't expected Mitch to extend his workday by attending the evening meeting. Once more she was impressed by his dedication.

"Good evening. For those of you I haven't met, I'm Mitch Jackson, the principal," he said, looking completely at ease in front of the crowd. "I'd like to welcome you to tonight's program and thank you for taking time out of your busy schedules to attend. I think you'll find it very worthwhile. As you know, we are extremely fortunate to have Chris Stevens on our staff, and even more fortunate that she agreed to make this presentation tonight. Let me review her credentials for you and I think you'll agree."

As he did so, the resonant, well-modulated timbre of his voice reflected both warmth and competence. Despite his casual attire of open-necked shirt and sport jacket, he radiated a quiet confidence and authority that marked him for leadership and engendered respect. He seemed to be a man in absolute control of his life, who had found his place in the world and had his act together, Tess reflected.

"And when Chris is finished, we'll both be happy to answer any questions you might have," he concluded, once again surprising Tess as he took a seat in the front row. Not only had he kicked off the meeting, he intended to be there when it finished. Did he always work such long hours? Tess wondered, filing the question away for the hoped-for interview. Since receiving the assignment that morning, she'd simply been too busy to call and discuss it with him. Perhaps she'd have a chance tonight, she mused. Though it would probably be difficult to single him out in this crowd.

An hour later, when the presentation ended, Tess realized she'd just spent one of the most worthwhile evenings of her life. Chris Stevens was good, just as Mitch had promised. She had touched on many of the fears and uncertainties that Tess had been feeling. Clearly Tess's experience with Bruce wasn't unique. But just as clearly, kids that age needed a strict set of rules and lots of one-on-one discussions with a caring adult. Chris had hammered home those points throughout her talk.

Which only made Tess realize just how remiss she'd been on both counts since coming to St. Louis. In Jefferson City, Bruce had never seemed to need rules; he'd just done the right thing without prompting and had always hung around with a wholesome group of friends. As for one-on-one talks, she'd never had to earmark certain times. They'd always eaten break-

fast and dinner together, so those talks had evolved
naturally.

Things had been different since they'd moved to
St. Louis. For one thing, since Tess was the new kid
on the block, her job schedule was somewhat erratic.
She was frequently assigned stories that required cov-
erage at undesirable times—evenings, weekends, holidays. As a result, dinners with Bruce were infrequent.
And he'd stopped eating breakfast, so that talk time
was gone, too. She'd also been too lax on rules.

Tess resolved to make some immediate changes,
both in her life and Bruce's. He wouldn't like it, but
if what Chris said was true—and Tess instinctively
sensed that it was—kids actually did better when
there was more rather than less parental intervention
in their lives. Not so much that you stifled them, but
enough to let them know that you cared deeply and
had standards by which you expected them to live. It
was clearly a tough line to walk, but Tess was determined to find it.

When the applause died down, Mitch stood and
rejoined Chris at the front of the room, and for another twenty minutes they adeptly answered questions, concluding with an invitation to stay for coffee
and a snack.

As Tess gathered up her purse and notebook, she
wearily glanced at her watch. Nine-thirty. It had been
another long day. Late in the afternoon she'd had to
cover a story that had run much longer than she expected, and she'd come to the meeting directly from
there. Her stomach rumbled ominously, reminding her
that she hadn't eaten anything since lunch, when
she'd grabbed some yogurt and an apple. She gazed

longingly toward the coffee table, where a crowd was now gathering. Sweets weren't exactly a healthy dinner, but she knew by the time she got home she'd be too tired even to nuke a microwave dinner, let alone eat it. A cookie or two would have to suffice, she decided.

The food line inched along slowly, and by the time she reached the table the crowd had thinned considerably. She hesitated at the display of sweets, debating the merits of chocolate chip versus oatmeal cookies, when a deep, rich chuckle distracted her.

"Take both. I am."

She turned to find Mitch smiling at her, and her heart did a little somersault.

"Are you planning to eat and run, or would you like to sit for a minute?" he asked.

Tess looked at him in surprise. "I, uh, hadn't actually thought about it."

"Well, I for one don't do especially well when I have to juggle coffee in one hand and food in the other. Seems like you need a third hand to eat. Would you like to join me over there?" He nodded toward a couple of unoccupied chairs against the back wall.

"Sure."

"I'll get the coffee. Just pile some cookies on a plate, and I'll meet you," he said, flashing her a grin as he headed for the coffeepot at the other end of the table.

Tess automatically did as he asked while she tried to figure out why he had approached her. Had something else happened with Bruce? she suddenly wondered in panic. After tonight's presentation, it was clear that she'd made some bad mistakes. And she intended to correct them. But maybe it was too late. Maybe Bruce had done something that...

"You must be hungry," Mitch teased, interrupting her train of thought as he settled into the folding chair beside her.

Tess glanced down, and a flush rose on her cheeks at the sight of the tall pile of cookies on her plate. "Good heavens, I don't know what I was thinking," she said faintly.

"Don't worry, I can help you put a dent in them," Mitch assured her as he handed her a cup of coffee and reached for a cookie. "Dinner was a long time ago. Probably for you, too."

"Actually, this *is* dinner," she admitted with a wry smile as she reached for a chocolate chip cookie.

He frowned. "Seriously?"

"Yes. I don't make a habit of this, but some days there just doesn't seem to be time to eat."

His frown deepened as his discerning gaze briefly swept over her. Last time he'd seen her she'd worn a boxy pantsuit that revealed little of her figure. Tonight she had on an oversize sweater that again effectively hid her curves. But her slender hands and the clearly defined bone structure in her face suggested to him that his original assessment of her as slender might need to be modified to too thin.

Tess was embarrassingly aware of his discreet perusal and sought to divert his attention. "I have a feeling you know what it's like to be time-challenged," she remarked. "You've obviously had a long day, too."

His gaze returned to her face. "True. But I *always*

find time to eat,'' he added with an engaging smile as he bit into his cookie.

He wasn't bringing up his reason for singling her out, Tess realized. Perhaps he was trying to lead up to it gradually, as he had in his office. But at this point she preferred the bad news up front. She took a steadying breath and gazed at him directly.

''Has something else happened with Bruce, Mr. Jackson?''

Mitch noted her tense grip on the coffee cup and looked at her quizzically. ''Not that I know of.''

Her brow wrinkled in puzzlement. ''Then why…? I mean, there are a lot of people here who would probably like to talk with you, so…well, I guess when you took me aside I just assumed that there was a problem,'' she finished, flustered.

Mitch looked at the woman across from him, a faint frown marring his own brow. Why *had* he sought her out? If he'd had any sense he would have left as soon as the group of parents around him had dispersed. He was beat, and the weekend ahead at his uncle's farm would be taxing. In fact, he'd planned to make his exit as quickly as possible. So what was it about Tess Lockwood that had made him suddenly change his mind when he'd seen her in line for coffee?

For one thing, she'd been on his mind a lot since their meeting, he admitted. Though he'd tried, he hadn't been able to explain—or dismiss—the odd effect she'd had on him that day. He'd gone to sleep more than once with her vivid but troubled green eyes as his last conscious image. It was oddly unsettling, considering that over the past few years he'd built up a pretty thick skin when it came to women. Yet somehow Tess had gotten under it. But he couldn't very well say that, he realized, struggling to come up with a suitable response.

"I figured you wouldn't know anyone here, and I wanted to make sure you felt welcome," he replied at last, striving for a conversational tone.

"Oh. Well, I appreciate that. And thank you for telling me about the program. It was very good."

"Chris does a terrific job," he agreed, relieved to be back on safer ground.

Tess suddenly realized that this was as good a time as any to broach the subject of the interview, so she took a deep breath and plunged in.

"You both do. In fact, I understand that you've just won the governor's award for excellence in education."

He looked at her in surprise. "How did you know?"

"It came over the wire at the newspaper where I work."

"Ah. No secrets from the press, I guess."

"Actually, the write-up wasn't very detailed."

He shrugged. "It was enough for most people."

"That's not what my editor thinks."

He eyed her speculatively. "What do you mean?"

"She'd like me to do a feature story on you."

He took a moment to respond, and she was suddenly afraid that he was going to turn her down flat. Instead, his reply was noncommittal. "I usually stay away from publicity."

"So we've heard," she admitted. "But when I mentioned that we'd met, my boss was hoping you might agree to talk with me. She thought you might feel more comfortable with a familiar face."

Mitch took a slow sip of his coffee as he considered the request. Frankly, he wasn't all that comfortable— with the story or the woman. He was a private person, for good reason. Few people knew the painful details of his past. Few people *needed* to know. He'd have to sidestep a lot of questions if he agreed to this interview, and that could be uncomfortable. So would being one-on-one with Tess Lockwood. She had already touched his heart in places that were best left undisturbed, and he barely knew her. Further contact could only be more disruptive to his peace of mind.

At the same time, he suspected that she was working hard to build a new career and a new life in St. Louis. Having to go back to her editor and say that she'd failed to nab an interview couldn't be good for her. It would just add more stress to what already appeared to be a stress-filled life. And he couldn't bring himself to do that.

"All right, Ms. Lockwood. Let's give it a try," he agreed.

Tess smiled. There was relief—and something else he couldn't quite identify—in her eyes. "Thank you."

"Call me tomorrow and we'll set something up. I may live to regret this, but at least the school board will be happy," he said with a lopsided grin.

"So will my editor." She shifted her purse onto her shoulder, and Mitch reached over to relieve her of her plate and cup.

"I'll take care of these."

"Thanks. And thank you again for telling me about

this meeting. And for agreeing to the interview.'' She tilted her head and gave him a rueful smile. ''I guess I'll be in your debt big time.''

He smiled, and his gaze deepened and connected with hers in a way that left her a bit breathless. ''I'll remember that.''

For a moment she actually felt lost in his eyes, and the buzz of voices around her seemed to recede. It was only with great effort that she finally dragged her gaze away from his, mumbled goodbye and beat a hasty retreat.

As Tess made her way to her car, she tried to figure out what had just happened. Or, more accurately, she tried to figure out *if* anything had happened. She'd probably read far too much into a simple look, she told herself. After all, there was nothing about her to rate any special attention. She was just one more parent with a troubled teen. Bruce was Mitch's main concern. And that was exactly as it should be.

Tess knew that. And accepted it. But it didn't stop a sudden surge of bittersweet longing from echoing softly in her heart.

# Chapter Three

"How about a cup of coffee to go with that pie?"

Mitch looked up at the older man and smiled. "You spoil me, Uncle Ray."

"No such thing. Your visits give me a good excuse to visit the bakeshop in town. Course, their pies aren't as good as Emma's. But they're sure a sight better'n mine."

"I do miss Aunt Emma's pies," Mitch agreed.

"Me, too. And a whole lot more," Uncle Ray said, his eyes softening briefly before he turned away to fiddle with the coffeemaker.

Mitch glanced at his uncle, still spare and straight at seventy-six. Only a pronounced limp, the result of a bad fracture from a severe fall over two years before, had slowed him down. Mitch knew the older man found the limp burdensome, though he never complained. And he still tried to put in a full day in the fields. Mitch had been trying to convince him to slow down, but as Uncle Ray always reminded him, farming was his life. He liked working the land.

Besides, Mitch reflected, the land had been the one constant in a life that had known its share of loss and grief. So he couldn't bring himself to force the issue. Instead, he'd found a job in St. Louis and spent his spare time helping out on the farm. It was the least he could do for the man who had been his lifeline six years before, who had shown him the way out of darkness step by painful step, who had helped him reconnect with his faith and find solace in the Lord. He owed his life—and his sanity—to Uncle Ray, and whenever the work began to overwhelm him, he only had to think back to that nightmare time to realize just how deeply in debt he was to this special man.

"So what's on the schedule this weekend?" Mitch asked when the older man turned to place a cup of coffee in front of him.

"There are still a couple of fields that need to be turned over," Uncle Ray said as he sat down across from Mitch. "I figured I'd get to them during the week, but I don't move quite as fast as I used to."

Mitch frowned. "I thought we agreed that we'd do the heavy work together, on weekends?"

Uncle Ray shrugged. "I have time to spare, Mitch. You don't. What little free time you have shouldn't be spent out here on an isolated farm with an old man."

"We've been through this before, Uncle Ray. I told you, I like coming out here. It's a nice change of pace from the city."

"Can't argue with that. It is a great place. Nothing beats the fresh air and open spaces. But you need some time to yourself, son. Companions your own age. You aren't going to find those things out here."

"I have everything I need," Mitch assured him. "My life is full. I have no complaints."

Uncle Ray looked at him steadily. "You know I don't interfere, Mitch. I learned my lesson on that score the hard way years ago." A flicker of sadness echoed in his eyes. "But I care about you, son. I don't want you to be alone."

Mitch reached over and laid his hand over his uncle's slightly gnarled fingers. "I'm not alone."

"That's not what I mean."

Mitch sighed. "I know. But I had my chance once, Uncle Ray. And I threw it away."

"You're a different man now."

"Maybe. Maybe not. I can't risk it."

"Well, it's your life, Mitch. I can't tell you how to live it. I just want you to be happy."

"I am happy, Uncle Ray."

"Can I ask you one other thing?"

"Sure." Mitch's reply was swift and decisive. In a friendship forged in pain, there were few secrets and even fewer off-limit questions.

"In all these years, has there ever been anyone…special in your life?"

Mitch took a sip of his coffee and forced his lips into a smile. "I assume you mean a woman."

"That's what I had in mind."

Mitch thought of all the women he'd met in the past six years who had made it clear that they were available if he was interested. But he hadn't been. Not even remotely. Not after… His pretense of a smile faded and he shook his head.

"No."

"Hmm." Uncle Ray pondered that for a moment as he scooped up another bite of pie. "So no one's ever caught your fancy, made you second-guess your decision to stay single?"

For some disconcerting reason the image of Tess Lockwood suddenly came to mind, and Mitch frowned. How odd. He barely knew the woman. They weren't even on a first-name basis. True, she'd somehow managed to touch a place in his heart that he'd carefully protected all these years. But it had to be just some weird quirk. What else could it be when they were essentially strangers? Mitch looked over at his uncle to find the older man gazing at him quizzically.

"What's wrong, son?"

Mitch shook his head. "For some strange reason the mother of one of my problem students just came to mind."

"A friend of yours?"

"Hardly. We've only met twice. She's a single mom who's got her hands full with a troublesome teen and a new job. I'm not sure why I thought of her just now."

"The mind works in mysterious ways," Uncle Ray said noncommittally. "Well, I just don't want to take up all of your free time. I can try to find one of the local boys to help me out."

"We've been down that road before," Mitch reminded him. "They're either all working on their family's farm or they don't know one end of a plow from the other."

"Good help is hard to find," Uncle Ray conceded.

"So let's just go on as we have been," Mitch concluded, savoring the last mouthful of pie. "It works for both of us. You get a farmhand, I get three square meals and fresh air, and we both get great conversation." He wiped his mouth and grinned as he laid his napkin on the table. "And if you ask me, that's a pretty good deal all the way around."

*The building was hot. And still. And ominous. A prickle of apprehension skittered across the back of his neck, and he tightened his hold on the gun. Something was wrong. Very wrong. He could sense it. And he'd been a cop long enough to respect his senses. Especially in abandoned warehouses.*

*At least he wasn't alone. Jacobsmeyer was circling in the other direction, only a shout away. And his partner was good. The best. Mitch drew a deep breath. Whatever was wrong, they'd find it. And fix it.*

*He stopped at a closed storage door, listening intently. Nothing. He tried the knob. Unlocked. Carefully he eased it open. Darkness. An even stronger feeling of foreboding. He swept the beam of his flashlight over the floor. Trash. Empty cans. A sport shoe protruding from a pile of boxes. A beat-up shopping cart. Some... He suddenly went still, then slowly swung his light back to the shoe, his stomach clenching. God, let me be wrong! he prayed. But his eyes hadn't lied. The shoe was attached to a leg.*

*He sucked in his breath, his heart hammering in his chest. He'd been here before, and it was never pretty. But it was his job. Steeling himself, he picked his way over the trash to the boxes. Hesitated. Took*

*another breath. Slowly let the arc of light travel up
the body. Hesitated again. Finally moved it up to the
face. Felt his world tilt. Crash. Shatter into a thou-
sand pieces. And then he screamed. And screamed
again. And again. And...*

Mitch jerked bolt upright in bed, shaking violently.
Dear God, the nightmare was back. Just when he'd
begun to believe that it had released its hold on him.
But now it had returned, stronger than ever.

"Mitch? You okay?"

Uncle Ray's concerned voice came from the other
side of the door, and Mitch sucked in a ragged breath.
"Yeah. I'm...fine," he called hoarsely, his voice as
tattered as his nerves.

"You need anything?" Though his uncle's voice
was calm, it was laced with worry.

Mitch took another deep breath, forcing air into
lungs that didn't want to expand. "No. I'm okay, Uncle Ray. Sorry I woke you."

"I wasn't really sleeping anyway. Try to go back
to sleep."

"Yeah, I will. Thanks."

Slowly Mitch eased himself back down, damp with
sweat. He'd put his uncle through this drill more
times than he could count. But the older man never
seemed to mind. He'd been through his own hell. He
understood.

Mitch wanted to let go of the nightmare. Wanted
to find a way to put it behind him and move on, as
Uncle Ray had. He'd always hoped that in time the
memory would fade. But he was less and less convinced that it would. Because while both men shared

a legacy of regret, only Mitch's included an unspeakable horror.

And no matter what he had done in the intervening years to make amends, no matter how often he'd prayed for release from the guilt and the pain, deep in his heart he knew that he didn't deserve a reprieve from the traumatic memory of that night.

At the sound of a knock, Mitch looked up. "Come in."

Karen opened the office door. "Ms. Lockwood is here."

Mitch glanced at his watch, then at his piled-high desk. As usual, the day had flown by and he'd finished only half of what he'd set out to accomplish. "There aren't enough hours in the day, Karen," he lamented with a sigh.

"That's because you take on too much."

He leaned back in his chair and steepled his fingers. "True," he conceded agreeably. "But what do you suggest I eliminate from my schedule? Tony Watson, who's picked me for the father figure he so desperately needs? The live teen chat room I host twice a week? The meetings with parents of problem kids? The budget?" He paused and tilted his head thoughtfully. "Actually, I could do without the budget, but I don't think the school board would approve."

Karen made a face. "I see your point."

He smiled and leaned forward again. "I thought you would. Okay, show Ms. Lockwood in. I might as well get this over with."

She hesitated and looked at him quizzically. "In

the interest of curiosity, how in the world did she get you to agree to this? You hate publicity.''

He shrugged. ''I guess she caught me at a weak moment.''

Karen planted her hands on her hips. ''You don't have weak moments.''

''Has anyone ever told you that you're an opinionated woman?'' he teased.

She tilted her head thoughtfully and counted off on her fingers. ''Let's see. My mother. My husband. My kids. The guy at the car repair shop. The director of the—''

''Enough!'' Mitch interrupted with a laugh. ''Just show Ms. Lockwood in.''

Karen grinned. ''You got it, boss.''

Mitch smiled and shook his head as he repositioned the stacks of papers on his desk. He'd inherited Karen when he'd taken on this job, and she'd been a godsend, serving as secretary, administrative assistant, sounding board, reality check and mother hen all rolled into one. Not to mention comic relief. He couldn't have gotten along without her.

''I hope that smile is a good omen for our interview.''

Mitch glanced up, and the perfunctory greeting died on his lips. He knew the woman in the doorway was Tess Lockwood. He would recognize those eyes anywhere. But everything else about her was different. Her hair hung loose and free, softly brushing her shoulders. She was wearing makeup—not much, but enough to enhance her already lovely features. And her clothes—gone were the boxy suit and baggy sweater. They'd been replaced by a short-sleeved silk blouse that clung to her curves and a sleek black A-line skirt that emphasized her trim waist and shapely legs. The transformation was stunning.

The seconds ticked by, and Mitch suddenly realized that he was staring. A hot flush of embarrassment crept up his neck, and he cleared his throat, struggling to recover.

"Come in, make yourself comfortable," he said, gesturing toward the chairs they'd occupied at their first meeting.

Tess made her way across the room, well aware of Mitch's reaction to her new look, though he'd recovered admirably. But while that brief, slightly dazed expression had done wonders for her ego, she suddenly regretted her impulsive purchase of the stylish new outfit. She'd been out of the dating game far too long to remember the rules, she realized in panic. What if Mitch actually…well…*did* something about that look in his eyes? Like ask her out. What would she do then? Bruce already thought she'd sided with the enemy. She could imagine his reaction if Mitch and she saw each other socially. Her relationship with her son was strained as it was, especially after their long talk this weekend about the new house rules. Good heavens, what had she been thinking? she berated herself. She should have just stuck with her serviceable, if dowdy, wardrobe.

But as she sat down and turned to Mitch, her doubts and uncertainties melted in the warmth of his eyes.

"I hope you won't take offense if I say that you look especially nice today," he said as he sat across from her, intrigued by her becoming blush—a reaction more typical of a schoolgirl than a once-married woman.

The husky quality in his voice did odd things to her stomach. "No, not at all," she replied a bit breathlessly.

He leaned back and propped an ankle on his knee. "Okay. Where do we start? I'm new at this, so you're going to have to walk me through it step by step."

Tess smiled and reached for her notebook. She might not be comfortable in the role of desirable woman, but she was quite comfortable in the role of reporter. "I like to think of an interview as simply a conversation. Except I get to ask most of the questions. Why don't we start with the award? Tell me what led to it."

He did so easily, talking about the innovative intervention programs and one-on-one involvement he encouraged between students, parents, administration and teachers. Under Tess's astute questioning, he revealed his passionate commitment to the kids, his concern about societal pressures on teens and on the American family, and the satisfaction he found in his work.

"I'm impressed, Mr. Jackson," she said honestly. "The world could use more people who care so deeply. And I'm also curious. I understand that you were once a police officer—in Chicago, I believe. This is quite a career switch. What prompted you to make the change?"

Tess sensed his sudden, almost imperceptible withdrawal.

"I saw a lot on the street," he said carefully, his words slower and more guarded. "Almost always too late for prevention. I wanted to find a way to intervene earlier. This kind of work seemed to offer that opportunity.''

Tess's job had taught her to be attuned to nuances, and there were plenty here. There was something very important that he wasn't revealing, and she was both curious and intrigued. But pushing usually just made a wary subject back off more. And she didn't really need to go any deeper for this interview. So, regretfully, she moved on. ''What brought you to St. Louis?''

She could sense his slight easing of tension. ''My uncle. He has a farm about an hour south of St. Louis, and a little over two years ago he had a bad fall that left him with a limp. I came that summer to help, and when it was obvious that he'd need ongoing assistance with the farm, I got a job here.''

''You must have been there this weekend,'' she said with a smile.

He looked at her in surprise. ''How did you know?''

''Your tan. When I saw you Thursday, your face didn't have nearly as much color.''

He grinned. ''Your powers of observation are admirable, Ms. Lockwood. You're right. We worked in the fields this weekend. I spend most of my free time there, especially in the nice weather.''

''Any other family locally?''

''No.''

''How about back in Chicago?''

An intense flash of pain ricocheted across his eyes. ''No. My parents are both gone and my…my wife died seven years ago.''

Mitch frowned. He hadn't meant to say that. Hadn't intended to reveal anything about Dana. Wasn't sure why he had.

"I'm so sorry," Tess said softly, taken aback by that fleeting glimpse of anguish. "I had no idea...." Her voice faltered. She'd wondered about a wife, found it difficult to believe someone like Mitch would have remained single all these years, had speculated there might be a divorce in his past. But she hadn't expected this. "I didn't mean to bring up painful memories," she apologized.

He took a deep breath. "It's okay." And surprisingly, it was. It didn't hurt nearly as much to talk about it as he'd expected. "It was cancer. It hit out of the blue and, mercifully, took her quickly. But it was still a terrible thing to watch. For a long time afterward I was...lost." For a lot of reasons, he thought, his gut twisting.

"I can understand that," Tess empathized. "I went through something similar with my father five years ago." She paused and took a deep breath. "It's awful to watch someone you love slip away."

"Yes, it is. But it helps to have a support system. I had my mother and Uncle Ray. How about you?"

"I had Bruce. And my faith, which was a great comfort."

"What about Bruce's father?"

Tess looked at him in surprise. She almost brushed aside the question, but for some reason decided to answer it. "We divorced six years ago."

His gaze softened in sympathy. "I'm sorry, Tess. Divorce can sometimes be as painful as death."

"More so, in some ways," she said sadly. "And

don't be sorry. The divorce was long overdue.'' She tilted her head and forced herself to smile. ''Now, how did things get turned around? I thought we were talking about you?''

He grinned. ''You already know the story of my life.''

Hardly, she thought. The man across from her had secrets, which he clearly didn't intend to reveal, she realized. Besides, she had plenty of material for her story. It was time to wrap things up.

Tess smiled and closed her notebook. ''Well, at least enough for my story,'' she amended.

''You know, this wasn't nearly as bad as I expected,'' Mitch admitted as they both rose and walked toward the door.

''I'm glad to hear it.'' She paused on the threshold and turned to hold out her hand. ''And thank you. My editor will be very pleased.''

He smiled as he took her hand in a firm grip. ''I hope your readers will feel the same way. I'm afraid they might be bored by the story of a dull school principal.''

At first Tess thought he was kidding, but as they said their goodbyes she realized he was dead serious. Dull? she thought incredulously. Mitch Jackson? No way. Intriguing would be a more apt description, she decided as she walked down the hall. She'd thought that by the end of the interview she'd know all the important things about the principal. But she had a feeling that she'd barely scratched the surface of this fascinating man. Instead of satisfying her curiosity, today's interview had made her want to find out more.

Unfortunately, there wouldn't be much opportunity

for that, she admitted with a pang of regret. Any future contact with the principal would be related to Bruce. Because to Mitch, she was just another mother dealing with a problem child.

Except at the end of the interview he had called her "Tess," she realized suddenly, stopping abruptly. That was a good sign. Wasn't it? Didn't it mean he thought of her as a person in her own right, not just as a mother?

Tess wasn't sure. Wasn't even sure if she *wanted* him to think of her that way. It was too scary. And complicated. And probably unwise.

She knew all that intellectually. And accepted it.

But for some reason, her heart just wasn't listening.

"So how was your day?"

"Okay."

Tess sighed. So far the new dinner-hour-together rule hadn't spurred the conversation and sharing she'd hoped for with Bruce. It was the old "You can lead a horse to water..." scenario. And Bruce wasn't drinking. But she wasn't going to give up.

"Did you look into the art club?" she asked, trying again. Chris Stevens had run through a list of supervised after-school activities at the meeting, and Tess had suggested the club to Bruce, who'd always shown strong artistic aptitude and interest.

"They're a bunch of geeks."

"How do you know?"

At his disgusted look, she let it drop.

They ate in silence for a few moments before she worked up the courage to introduce a new subject. "Guess who I interviewed today?" she asked, her tone a little too bright. When he didn't respond, she plunged in. "Mr. Jackson."

That got his attention. "Why?"

"He just received the governor's award for excellence in education."

"You're kidding!"

"No. He's doing good work at the high school."

Bruce gave a disdainful snort. "Right."

"So you don't think he's a good principal?"

Bruce shrugged. "He's too 'in-your-face.'"

"Meaning?"

"He's always hanging around with the kids. And watching what we're doing. I thought principals were supposed to stay in their office and run the school."

"Maybe he's trying to change the rules."

"Why?"

"I asked him that in the interview."

"Yeah?" Bruce looked interested. "What did he say?"

"He said that when he was a cop, he saw a lot of kids on the street who were in trouble. But by the time the police got involved, it was usually too late. He said he wanted to find a way to help kids before they got to that point. That's why he became a principal. And why he's changing the rules, I expect."

"He was probably a better cop than he is a principal," Bruce said.

"Do all the kids think so?"

He shrugged. "The geeks seem to like him. The guys I hang around with don't. Except maybe Tony Watson. But he's got problems. I think he figures Mr. Jackson can help him."

"What kind of problems?"

"Stuff at home. His parents don't get along. I think his dad drinks, and his mom's never around. She travels a lot for her job."

"Doesn't sound too great," she agreed. "So what does Mr. Jackson do?"

"He just talks to him. After school sometimes. Tony seems to be okay for a while after that. But it never lasts long. I feel sorry for him."

"Maybe you could invite him over some time."

Bruce gave her another disgusted look and changed the subject. "I saw your name on the sign-up sheet for the food booth at the school carnival. Did you really volunteer?"

"Yes."

"Why?"

"I thought we could spend some time together there." Which was true enough. But she'd hoped it would also give her a chance to meet some of his elusive friends.

He looked appalled. "Mom! Even if I go, I was going to hang around with the guys."

"I don't expect you to spend the whole day with me, Bruce. But I thought we could have a hot dog and soda or something when I finish working. And what do you mean, *even* if you go?"

"I'm not sure about it. I have to check with the guys."

"But what do *you* want to do?" she pressed. "You used to like carnivals, especially the rides."

He shrugged. "That's kid stuff."

*But that's what you are!* she wanted to cry out. *Just a kid.* Instead, she reached for his empty plate. "I don't know. *I* still like carnivals, and I'm no kid,'' she said, striving for a conversational tone.

He considered that. ''Well, I might go. For a while.''

''I hope so. It would be fun. And you know what else I was thinking? Maybe this weekend we could go to the art museum. I hear it's great, and there's an exhibit right now that I thought you might especially like. It's on the—''

''I'll have a lot of homework this weekend,'' Bruce cut her off.

''You have to have some time for fun, too.''

''Joe's having a party Saturday night at his house. Maybe I could go to that,'' he said hopefully.

''Maybe. Will his parents be home?''

''Oh, Mom!''

''Yes or no?''

''I don't know.''

''If you give me his phone number, I'll call and check.''

''Forget it.'' He shoved his chair back and stood. ''Can I dry the dishes later?''

''Sure.''

Tess sighed as he disappeared down the hall. So far, she didn't seem to be making much progress. But things would change eventually. She was sure of it.

She only hoped the change would be for the better.

# *Chapter Four*

If she never saw another funnel cake in her life it would be too soon, Tess concluded, wrinkling her nose in distaste as she poured the batter through the namesake cooking implement and watched it coil around unappetizingly in the hot grease. After making the fat-laden sweets for the past hour, Tess couldn't believe that anyone would actually eat them. But they'd been selling like the proverbial hot cakes to the students at the school carnival.

Tess lifted the golden, cooked pastry onto a paper plate and liberally sprinkled it with powdered sugar before handing it to the parent who was filling orders at the front counter. She glanced at her watch, noting with relief that her shift was almost over. In ten minutes she'd be free to have the agreed-upon hot dog and soda with Bruce.

*If* he showed up, she amended, her worried gaze scanning the school grounds. So far he'd made himself scarce. Since their arrival she'd caught only a fleeting glimpse of him in the distance, and his friends were nowhere to be seen. So much for any hopes she'd harbored about meeting his elusive companions, she conceded with a resigned sigh.

"How's business?"

The familiar, husky voice close to her ear made her jump, and she dropped the funnel into the vat, gasping in pain as hot grease splattered and sizzled on the back of her hand. She heard Mitch's startled oath, and a moment later he ducked under the rail and took her hand, cradling it in his as he frowned at the shiny red patch of burned skin.

"This needs attention." His gaze met hers, contrite and troubled. "I'm sorry, Tess."

There was something about the way he said her name, his voice roughened with some emotion she couldn't identify, that made her own voice quaver.

"It—it wasn't your fault," she assured him. "If I'd been paying more attention this never would have happened. And I'm fine, really."

Instead of responding, Mitch called over her shoulder, "Hank, Tess burned her hand. She needs to go to first aid."

The older man in charge of the booth joined them, a concerned look on his face. "A casualty already?"

"It's nothing, really," Tess insisted, trying to tug her hand free. But when it was obvious that Mitch didn't intend to release it, she stopped struggling.

Hank peered down at the injury with a troubled expression and seconded Mitch's diagnosis. "That's a bad burn. You go on, Tess. We have plenty of help. And your replacement will be here any minute."

Tess glanced down at her hand. The burn did look

nasty. But she found herself focusing more on Mitch's strong, capable fingers and his tender touch, which were playing havoc with her respiration. She forced herself to take a long, steadying breath before she spoke. "All right. You both win. Where's the first aid station?"

Mitch's hand dropped to the small of her back and he guided her out of the booth. "I'll go with you."

Tess knew she should protest. She was perfectly capable of finding her own way. And Mitch was a busy man. But she liked the feel of his hand at her waist, even if it was just a polite, impersonal gesture. Tess couldn't remember the last time she'd been touched in such a protective way. And whatever Mitch's intent, his touch satisfied a need deep inside her, one that often surfaced during the long, solitary nights, or when the demands of single parenthood overwhelmed her. It was a touch that made her feel as if she wasn't quite so alone. As if someone cared. That feeling, long absent from her life, was one to be savored, if only for a brief moment.

"Here we are. It's not exactly the Mayo Clinic, but they should be able to handle this," Mitch said with a smile, putting an end to her momentary flight of fantasy.

The school nurse quickly saw to the burn, and within a couple of minutes Tess was free to go.

"Can I buy you a soda?" Mitch asked as he lifted the flap for her to precede him out of the tent.

Tess's heart gave a little leap, and an inexplicable feeling of happiness washed over her. "You don't have to do that," she protested halfheartedly.

He flashed her a crooked grin. "True. But I'd like

to. After all, you were hurt, in part, because of me. It's the least I can do.''

So his offer was just part of the job. Tess's spirits quickly nose-dived, but she forced her lips into a smile. ''I'm sure you have other things to attend to, Mr. Jackson. But thank you.''

Mitch almost accepted her answer at face value—as a brush-off. He wasn't the type to force his company on anyone, man or woman. But for some reason he hesitated. Her refusal somehow didn't ring true. In his gut he sensed that she *wanted* to spend more time with him. So what was holding her back?

For a long moment he studied the woman across from him. Today she was dressed in form-fitting jeans and a cotton T-shirt that softly hugged her curves. She had the body of a twenty-year-old, Mitch noted appreciatively—not to mention gorgeous eyes. A man could drown in their delicious green depths. But there was hurt in them, too, and wariness. Tess Lockwood struck him as a woman who had learned through adversity to be strong and capable and independent, who was used to tackling the challenges of life single-handedly. But he also sensed that somewhere deep inside she yearned to be less alone. Not that she needed a man to lean on. Just that she would welcome someone with whom to share the triumphs and tragedies of life. Yet something—or someone—had made her cautious. Unsure. Even a little skittish. It was uncertainty, not unwillingness, that was holding her back from accepting his invitation, Mitch suspected. So he decided to make one more attempt.

He stuck his hands into the back pockets of his jeans and gave her his most persuasive smile. ''First of all, the name is Mitch. I believe I've been calling you Tess for quite some time, so turnabout is fair play. And second, I don't have anything else to attend to. So would you reconsider?''

Tess's breath caught in her throat, and her spirits rebounded. He really did want to spend more time with her! He wasn't just being polite! The warmth and sincerity in his disarming smile convinced her of that. She drew a deep, unsteady breath and nodded. ''All right. Thank you.''

His smile broadened. ''Good. I hate to drink alone.''

A couple of minutes later, sodas in hand, they found a table in the sun. Tess closed her eyes and lifted her face to the balmy rays, enjoying their caressing warmth.

''Mmm. This is great,'' she said, her lips curving into an appreciative smile.

Mitch took a sip of his soda and let his gaze rest on those lips—soft and supple and made to be kissed. She was more relaxed than he'd ever seen her—and far more appealing than was healthy for either of them, he realized with a start as his gaze swept down the slender column of her throat and lingered on the bare expanse of creamy skin at her collarbone. He swallowed with difficulty and looked away, firmly reminding himself that he wasn't in the market for romance. And neither was the lady, from all indications.

When he glanced back she was looking at him, her chin propped in one hand, her slender fingers playing with the soda straw. ''You got lucky, you know that?'' she remarked with a smile.

Her words jolted him momentarily, until common

sense kicked in. Tess couldn't possibly be talking about the fact that they'd met—even if that was the first thought that had come to *his* mind. "How so?" he asked, striving for a casual tone.

"The weather," she replied matter-of-factly. "Mid-March can be awfully nasty in Missouri. It takes a lot of courage to plan an outdoor carnival for this time of year."

He let his breath out slowly, willing his racing pulse to slow down. "Not courage," he corrected her. "Tradition. Southfield High's been having this carnival on the same weekend for years. And I think they've only had bad weather once."

"Well, someone's doing something right. But I was surprised to see you here. I thought you went to your uncle's on weekends."

"I do. I'm heading out there as soon as I leave here. But I had to put in an appearance."

Tess's fingers stilled and she frowned. "So I *am* holding you up."

He shook his head. "I wasn't going to leave until after—"

He broke off abruptly to look over Tess's shoulder, and she turned to find Bruce glaring at her.

"I waited by the food booth for ten minutes," her son said accusingly, shooting a venomous glance at Mitch.

A crestfallen look swept over Tess's face. "Oh, honey, I'm sorry!" she apologized contritely. "I burned my hand and Mit…Mr. Jackson walked me over to first aid. We stopped to have a soda on the way back. I just lost track of the time."

He shrugged stiffly. "It doesn't matter. The food

here stinks, anyway. I'd rather go out with the guys for pizza. If that's okay.''

Mitch saw the distress on Tess's face and stood. "I was just leaving," he said easily. "Why don't you stay and have something to eat with your mom, Bruce?''

Bruce glared at him. "I don't have to do what you say when I'm not in school.''

"Bruce!" Tess reprimanded him, shocked by his defiant tone. "Apologize to Mr. Jackson!''

"Why? I didn't do anything wrong," he countered sullenly.

Tess rose, bristling with anger. "You most certainly did. You were rude and insolent. There was no call for that tone. I raised you better than that. Now, apologize.''

Their gazes locked for a moment in a silent battle of wills. But though they were equal in height, he was no match for her maternal authority. At last his gaze fell and he studied the toe of his sport shoe.

"I'm sorry," he mumbled begrudgingly, refusing to meet Mitch's eyes. Then he looked at Tess. "So can I go with the guys for pizza?''

Tess debated silently. She'd blown it just now by not showing up on time for the "date" with her son. And she'd added insult to injury by allowing Bruce's nemesis to be the cause of her tardiness. She needed to make it up to him, and this might be the way. After all, his request wasn't unreasonable. And she had been keeping him on a pretty tight leash. She longed to turn to Mitch, ask his advice, but that would only make things worse with Bruce. She was on her own.

"Where are they going?" she stalled.

"Just down the street. To Little Italy."

Tess knew the place. It was a popular—and safe—hangout for high school kids. "Okay. But I want you home by seven."

"Seven! But Mom, it's Saturday night!"

"And you're fourteen." She ignored his dirty look. "Do you want me to pick you up?"

His expression said, "Get real," but his spoken words were different. "I can walk."

The restaurant was only a few blocks from their apartment and the area was safe, so Tess nodded. "Okay. I'll see you at seven. No later, Bruce. Got it?"

"Yeah."

Tess watched as he disappeared into the crowd, then turned to Mitch, her shoulders drooping. "So did I blow it?" she asked heavily, clearly distressed by the confrontation.

He shook his head. "You can't keep kids under lock and key all the time. And you can't always be there to watch over their shoulder. Little Italy is okay. And you set a clear curfew. You did the right thing, Tess."

She wanted to believe him. Desperately. She'd made a lot of mistakes in her life, but she was determined not to make any more when it came to Bruce. Mitch's reassurance was comforting. But more important, it was credible. He wasn't the type to lie just to make someone feel good. Especially when a kid's future was at stake. She'd learned enough about him to know that. The knot in her stomach eased slightly and she slowly exhaled. "Thanks."

Mitch glanced at his watch, and Tess took the cue.

She reached for her purse and slung it over her shoulder. "Thanks for the soda, too. I'm sure you're anxious to get on the road."

Her statement was true enough. Mitch had planned to arrive at the farm before dark. He could still make it if he left now.

"Actually, since your meal plans fell apart, I thought maybe we could grab a bite first. The food here isn't quite as bad as Bruce implied."

Judging by the faint flush that rose on her cheeks, the invitation surprised her as much as it did him.

"I don't want to hold you up," she said hesitantly.

She'd given him an out. Which he should take, he told himself firmly. Spending time with an attractive mother of a problem student wasn't in his plans. Nor was it safe. He knew that at some intuitive level. The logical thing to do was grab a carryout and take off. But somehow his heart wasn't listening to logic.

"We both have to eat anyway. Unless you make a habit of cookies for dinner."

She smiled. "No. That was a rare exception. I much prefer real food."

"Two orders of real food coming up, then. What would you like?"

"Surprise me."

"No hated foods I should steer clear of?"

She grinned. "Only funnel cakes."

He chuckled, a deep sound that resonated pleasantly in her ears. "I don't blame you. Okay, sit tight and I'll be right back."

When he returned a few minutes later laden with bratwurst, potato salad, coleslaw and brownies, Tess arched her eyebrows. "So did you invite everyone in line to join us?" she teased.

"Hey, we eat hearty on the farm," he countered as he divided up the food. "You need a lot of energy to drive tractors and mend fences and pitch hay."

"So what excuse do *I* have for eating all these calories?"

His gaze swept over her, swift but discerning. "I don't think you need to worry."

Though his tone was matter-of-fact, his words caused an odd flutter in her stomach. She watched him surreptitiously, admiring his strong profile as he squeezed mustard onto his bratwurst. He was a man who could easily let his good looks go to his head, could take advantage of his innate charisma. Instead, he was down-to-earth and genuine. Though he was clearly used to being in charge, his authority was tempered by kindness—and something else she couldn't quite put her finger on. But it was there, in his eyes. Something had happened to Mitch Jackson somewhere along the way that had changed him irrevocably. Tess knew that as suddenly and surely as she knew that for the first time in years she actually found herself attracted to a man.

At just that moment Mitch looked at her, and she felt herself dissolving in the warmth of his dark brown eyes. A sudden surge of longing swept over her, setting off warning bells in the recesses of her heart and sending shock waves rippling through her. For a woman who thought she'd tamed her physical needs, who had convinced herself that she'd built up an immunity to their power, it was extremely disconcerting to discover that it had simply taken the right man to reawaken her long-dormant desire. The fact that she wasn't in the market for romance—nor, she suspected, was he—didn't seem to matter. The attraction was real and seemed to have a life of its own, which scared her. And made her want to turn and flee. In fact, she intended to do just that at the first opportunity. In the meantime, she needed to focus on something else.

"So tell me about the farm. How big is it?" she asked, grasping at the first thought that came to mind.

If Mitch was surprised by the abrupt change of subject, or noticed the slightly breathless quality of her voice, he didn't let on. "It's a nice spread," he replied easily. "About five hundred acres. Uncle Ray leases most of it to a tenant farmer now, but he still works about a hundred acres. It's enough to keep us busy."

"Do you spend all your free time there?"

He shrugged. "Pretty much. It's a nice change of pace."

"I have some friends who own a farm near Jefferson City," Tess told him. "It's smaller than your uncle's—probably a couple hundred acres, mostly fields, some woods. Bruce and I used to go out there sometimes on the weekends. He always enjoyed it. Of course, that was in the old days. I doubt that a farm would hold much appeal for him now. It wouldn't be cool." She sighed. "It seems like sometimes…sometimes I hardly know him anymore," she confessed in a disheartened tone.

Her face grew sad and forlorn, and Mitch fought a powerful impulse to reach over and take her hand. He deliberately reached for the potato salad instead.

"Adolescence is tough on everyone," he commiserated, purposely adopting a clinical tone. "But most kids get through it unscathed. Some just need a little more help than others."

Tess nodded. "Like Bruce. How do you spot kids like him?"

He shrugged. "I pay attention, especially to midterm transfers. They often have problems adjusting and finding their niche. It's not rocket science."

"No. It's more difficult than rocket science," Tess declared emphatically. "Because human beings aren't as predictable as rockets. Especially adolescents."

"They can be just as volatile, though. But there are patterns of behavior that pretty consistently indicate trouble, if you know what to watch for."

"Which clearly you do. How did you learn so much about kids, Mitch?"

It was an innocent question. But his gut twisted painfully, and he found it difficult to swallow the bite of potato salad he'd just taken. They were dangerously close to off-limits territory, and he bought himself a moment to formulate an answer by taking a long, slow drink of his soda. "I was young once," he replied at last, aware that his response was incomplete and unsatisfactory. But it was all he was prepared to offer.

Before her reporter skills could kick in, prompting her to ask a follow-up question, he turned the tables. "You mentioned in our first meeting that Bruce has a problem with self-esteem. As Chris pointed out in the meeting you attended, self-image is a big part of what drives adolescent behavior. Kids who have issues in this area are often susceptible to peer pressure.

But it's a bit unusual to find that problem in teenagers who have at least one very loving, involved parent in their life—which Bruce does. It's more common when kids come from homes where the parents are apathetic or even abusive." He hesitated, and when he spoke again his tone was more personal than professional. "Can I ask you something, Tess?"

She broke off a piece of her brownie and let it crumble through her fingers. She knew where this was leading. Peter. She'd never talked about her relationship with her ex-husband—to anyone. Had never felt the need to dredge up those unhappy memories. Until now. Suddenly she wanted to share the trauma—at least some of it—with this man whose kind, sympathetic eyes seemed to invite confidences. *Please, Lord,* she prayed silently, *help me find the courage to share this hurt I've held so long in my heart. And the courage to trust my instincts about this man, who seems so compassionate and caring.*

Her heart thudding painfully in her chest, she drew a deep breath and spoke quietly. "You want to know about Bruce's father."

"I *have* wondered where he fits into the picture," Mitch admitted, his eyes watchful, his tone careful.

"He doesn't."

Mitch looked surprised. "There's no contact at all?"

"No. Unless he happens to remember to send a check to Bruce at Christmas. But the lack of contact isn't a negative in this case." Tess took another deep breath and gazed at him directly. "Peter—my ex-husband—was a lousy father. It's as simple as that. When we first got married, he said he didn't want children right away. When Bruce came along two years later—quite unexpectedly—I accepted it. Peter didn't. I thought he'd eventually come around, but he never did. He resented Bruce for intruding on our lives, and he held him to impossible standards. Bruce tried so hard to please him—'' her voice broke, and she forced herself to take a deep, steadying breath ''—but nothing he did was good enough. In the beginning I tried to make excuses for Peter, but kids are smart. Bruce knew how Peter felt about him. Yet he still kept trying to win his love. Only, Peter didn't have any to give—to Bruce or, as I finally realized, to me.''

The next part was even harder, and Tess dropped her gaze to stare at the mangled brownie on her plate. When she spoke her voice was so soft that Mitch had to lean closer to hear. ''I married Peter when I was twenty. He was the first man I'd ever seriously dated, and I mistook infatuation for love. He was handsome and ambitious and successful, and I was flattered when he took a fancy to me. It was only later that I realized what the real attraction was—my father's political contacts. Peter was a lobbyist for the theme park industry, and my dad was a state senator. He had the connections Peter wanted. I was just…just the means to an end.''

Even after so many years the admission hurt, and Tess paused to draw a shaky breath before venturing a look at Mitch. Instead of the pity she'd been afraid of finding in his eyes, she saw something else entirely. Something surprising. Anger. Controlled, but simmering just below the surface.

"He was an idiot." Mitch's voice was low, but intense.

Tess's eyes widened at the unexpected comment, but before she had time to analyze it, he spoke again. "How long were you married?"

"Too long. Ten years chronologically, but it felt like a lifetime. Frankly, our marriage began to deteriorate almost immediately, and it disintegrated after Bruce was born. But I kept hoping things would improve. Even when I went back to school to finish my degree, I still did all the things that were expected of the wife of someone in Peter's position. I kept thinking that if I just did a better job as a wife, he would learn to love me—and Bruce."

"I take it that never happened."

She shook her head sadly. "No. I stayed far longer than was healthy for anyone. We were all miserable. Not that anyone would have guessed. Peter put up a good front publicly. In his profession, it was in his best interest to keep up the pretense of being a solid family man." Tess gave a brief, bitter laugh. "What a joke. We were a family in name only."

"What finally made you decide to leave?"

Tess gazed at him, into eyes that beckoned her to open her heart and share her pain, to tell this final secret. She *wanted* to. Wanted to exorcise the ghosts of that final humiliation. But even now, years later, the words wouldn't come. The memory still hurt too much. No, she couldn't talk about that final degrading moment, the turning point when only one option had been left to her. Not even to this man, who she suspected would treat her disclosure with understanding and gentleness.

"I was worried about Bruce. About the damage that had already been done, and the damage that would continue to be done if we stayed. And Peter had an offer to move on to bigger things in Washington. The time was right for us to go our separate ways." Which was the truth. Just not the *whole* truth. But it was enough. For now.

Tess crumpled her napkin with hands that weren't quite steady and forcibly lightened her tone. "So now you don't have to wonder about Bruce's dad anymore. He's out of our life. Which is no great loss. And we're doing fine on our own. Better, really. I just wish I could erase the scars he left with Bruce. But I'm working on it."

And what about the scars he left with you? Mitch wondered silently. Though he suspected she would deny it, they were there. He could see them in the sadness and disillusionment in her eyes, which spoke eloquently of her own pain as well as the pain she felt on behalf of her son. Yet she had spunk. And spirit. And strength. She was a survivor. She had made a courageous decision, and then done what was required to create a new life for herself and Bruce. But she'd also clearly paid a price. In stress. Uncertainty. Tension. Emotional distress.

Mitch's throat tightened and he was again tempted to reach over and take her hand. Again he held back, afraid of where that simple touch could lead. He'd vowed years ago to stay away from personal involvements. Friend, adviser, counselor, confidant—he could handle those roles. But nothing more. Yet more was exactly what his heart wanted from Tess Lockwood. So he needed to keep his distance. For both their sakes.

"I'm sorry, Tess."

It was a simple but heartfelt comment. And it was all that needed to be said.

"Thanks. I am, too. Frankly, I never thought I'd end up being a single mom at thirty-six. I really believed in that 'till death do us part' vow we took before God, you know?"

The wistful note in her voice tugged at his heart, and he could no longer resist the temptation. He reached over and covered her hand with his. "Don't stop believing in it, Tess," he said huskily. "It can happen."

His gaze locked with hers, and for just a moment she stopped breathing. And started believing.

"Can I tell you something, Mitch?" she said impulsively, her throat tight with emotion.

"Of course."

"Your wife was one lucky woman."

Tess wasn't surprised that Mitch seemed taken aback by her personal comment. She was taken aback herself. But she *was* surprised by the raw pain that seared through his eyes. And by his response.

"Dana wasn't all that lucky, Tess," he said flatly. "Frankly, I wasn't the best husband."

She gave him a skeptical look. "I have a feeling you're being too hard on yourself."

He brushed her comment aside impatiently. "No. It's true. I was too caught up with being a cop, working long hours and weird shifts. I loved Dana—but my job always came first. And a lot of things suffered because of that.'' He gazed at her directly, his face somber. ''There are a lot of regrets in my past, Tess.''

''You don't have a corner on that market,'' she said gently. ''I guess all we can do is learn from our mistakes and move on.''

The ghost of a smile touched the corners of his lips. ''You sound like my uncle. He's always telling me the same thing.''

She smiled in return. ''And have you taken his advice?''

''I'm trying.''

''That's all any of us can do. That, and put our trust in the Lord. My faith was the one absolute in my life for a long time. Even when my world was falling apart, I knew that I wasn't alone.''

Mitch sighed. ''I wish I could say the same. There was a time in my life when I felt totally abandoned and lost. But thanks to my uncle, I found my way back to my faith. That's one of the things I'm most grateful to him for.''

''Speaking of your uncle...'' Tess reminded him gently.

Mitch glanced at his watch. There was no way he'd make the farm before dark. But somehow he didn't care. His gaze connected with hers again, and there was an intensity in his eyes, a message in their depths, that made her pulse suddenly trip into double time. ''He'll understand. Besides, can I tell you something, Tess? When it comes to regrets, the past hour with you isn't one of them. Except for that.'' He reached over and gently tapped the edge of the burn with a whisper-soft touch of his finger.

Tess gazed down, trying to still the staccato beat

of her heart. She couldn't very well say it, but she'd gladly burn the other hand for another hour with this special man. Not that it could ever lead anywhere, she reminded herself. Her first priority was Bruce, and the last thing she needed to do was complicate her relationship with her son by starting one with his enemy.

"I enjoyed it, too," she replied softly. "And the burn will heal."

But not her heart, she thought as they said goodbye. For just a brief moment she'd had a taste of something she'd never experienced, even in her marriage— a meeting of souls. She and Mitch had connected at some elemental level—physically, mentally, emotionally, spiritually. In other circumstances, there would be great promise in this relationship. But she had to put her relationship with Bruce first. And it didn't look as if she could have both. Which meant only one thing.

She would have to add yet another regret to her already long list.

# Chapter Five

By seven-thirty Tess was angry. By eight o'clock she was getting worried. When there was still no sign of Bruce by eight-thirty, she was beginning to panic.

And by the time the phone rang at nine o'clock, she was frantic. Her voice was shaking as she struggled with a simple hello.

"Ms. Lockwood?" The male voice was unfamiliar.

"Yes."

"This is Sergeant Roberts of the Southfield Police Department. We have your son here at the station. He was a passenger in a car that was involved in an accident."

Tess's stomach plummeted to her toes, and her lungs stopped working. "Is he all right?"

"He's scared. But not hurt. Only the driver was injured. A laceration above his eye that needed stitches. I'll be happy to give you the details when you come to get your son."

"I'll be there in fifteen minutes."

Tess replaced the receiver and sank onto a stool by the counter as her legs suddenly gave way. She forced herself to take a long, slow breath and then buried her face in her hands. She wanted to cry—with relief...frustration...anger...fear...and a depressing feeling of helplessness. She'd been afraid that Bruce was heading for a run-in with the law. But she'd hoped that she'd intervened in time to keep that from happening. At least this call wasn't related to law-breaking, she consoled herself. But the next time it very well could be—unless she quickly figured out a way to get her son to see the light and straighten up.

As it turned out, the summons to the police station wasn't quite as innocent as Tess had assumed. Sergeant Roberts was waiting when she arrived, and once she was seated across his desk he didn't waste any time getting to the point.

"Ms. Lockwood, are you aware that your son was drinking this evening?" he asked bluntly.

She stared at him, her eyes widening in shock. "What?"

The sergeant grunted and pulled a sheet of paper toward him. "I guess that answers my question." He consulted the document in front of him. "According to his statement, he and several friends went to Little Italy and got a take-out pizza, which they washed down with beer. Then they switched to gin and went cruising. Eventually they drove into a tree. The driver's blood alcohol level was well above the legal limit. Frankly, they got lucky. They could have killed someone. Or been killed themselves."

During the officer's recitation of the facts, Tess felt the color slowly drain from her face. When he finally looked up, his stern expression eased slightly and his voice lost its clinical tone.

"Would you like a drink of water?"

Tess shook her head jerkily. "No. Thanks." She took a deep breath and met the officer's gaze directly. She didn't want to ask the question, didn't want to believe it was possible, but she had to have all the facts.

"Was...was Bruce drunk, too?"

The man shook his head. "We could smell the gin on his breath. He claims he only took one drink of beer and a sip of the gin. Frankly, I'm inclined to believe him. We did a Breathalyzer, and he was clean."

Tess swallowed with difficulty and closed her eyes. Though he'd made some very bad choices, he'd somehow found the strength to temper his response to peer pressure when it came to drinking. *Thank You, Lord, for that,* she prayed fervently. But the police officer was right. Things could have been so much worse.

When she finally opened her eyes, the sergeant's gaze was more sympathetic. "Has he been in trouble before, Ms. Lockwood? Some of the other kids are familiar to us, but I don't recall seeing Bruce before."

"We've only been here since the first of the year. Bruce has had some adjustment problems at school, but I've been addressing them. I'd hoped we were making some progress, but..." Her disheartened voice died away.

The man frowned. "Look, ma'am, we see a lot of kids in here who are heading down the wrong path. But the fact that Bruce didn't drink with his buddies is a good sign. Trust me. It's tough to say no in that situation. I wouldn't give up on him yet.''

Tess sent him a grateful look and straightened her shoulders. ''Thank you. I don't plan to. Just the opposite, in fact. If he thought I was being tough before, he's in for a real shock now. Is he being charged with anything?''

He rose. ''Not this time. He was just a passenger, and the Breathalyzer was negative. But we put him in a holding cell. More for effect than anything else,'' the man said, flashing her a quick grin. ''I'll take you back. And just so you know, I read him the riot act and put the fear of God into him. I think it made an impact.''

He paused outside a door, entered a security code, then ushered Tess through. ''Do you want me to give you a few minutes back here, or just let him out?''

Tess looked around—at the sterile, unfriendly walls, the security cameras, the barred windows, the stripped-down furnishings. ''I'll take the few minutes back here,'' she said firmly.

He nodded and stopped beside another door with a small window. Tess glanced inside, and her heart contracted painfully. Bruce was huddled in the corner, sitting on a cot, hugging his knees to his chest. His head was down, and his shoulders were hunched and tense. She could almost feel his fear.

Sergeant Roberts fitted a key in the lock and swung the door open. ''He's all yours. I'll be back in fifteen minutes,'' he said quietly.

Tess took a deep breath and stepped inside. A moment later she heard the door shut and lock behind her. But her attention was focused on her son, who was now staring at her with wide, wary and very scared eyes. Her first impulse was to rush over to him, take him in her arms as she had when he was a child with a nightmare, and reassure him that everything would be all right. But he wasn't a child anymore. And this nightmare was real. As for everything being all right—she couldn't guarantee that. It wasn't in her power. *He* had to help. And so she held her ground silently, waiting for him to speak first.

After several long seconds he drew a shuddering breath. "Aren't you going to say anything?" he asked in a subdued tone.

Tess willed her voice to sound calm and in control, even if her insides were churning. "Like what?"

He shrugged. "I don't know. Mother stuff. Tell me it was wrong to miss the curfew. And to ride with the guys when they were drinking."

"You said it for me."

He sighed. "I guess I'm grounded for life."

"Certainly for the foreseeable future."

He looked at her steadily. "I just tasted the beer and only had one sip of gin."

"That's what the sergeant said you told him."

"It's true."

"How old are you, Bruce?"

He eyed her warily. "You know."

"And what's the legal drinking age?"

"I know what it is, Mom." He dropped his head to his knees and turned away.

Tess took another steadying breath and moved to the straight chair beside the cot, praying that she would find the right words, words that would make an impact on her son. At this proximity, she could

see the tearstains on his colorless face, and once more
she wanted to simply pull him into her arms and comfort him. But the time wasn't right. Not yet.

"Let me tell you something, Bruce. It took a lot of
guts not to drink more than a sip. Peer pressure can
be pretty powerful, and I admire you for saying no.
But that wouldn't have saved your life if the accident
had been worse. You needed to say no sooner. Drinking and driving don't mix. You know that. Fortunately, only the driver was injured. And his stitches
will be out in a couple of weeks. But he won't get
rid of his juvenile record so easily."

Bruce turned to her, and she saw the fear in his
eyes intensify. "Are the police going to...to book
me?"

Tess let him sweat it out for a moment before she
shook her head. "No."

His relief was palpable. "So I can go home?"

"Yes. But take a look around you while we wait
for the sergeant to come back, Bruce. And remember
it. Because whether or not you end up back here is
up to you."

Bruce studied the small cell, distaste written all
over his face. And when they finally heard the key
being inserted in the lock, he was on his feet instantly.

Sergeant Roberts opened the door and then silently
escorted them back to the reception area.

Tess held out her hand. "Thank you, Sergeant."

He took her fingers in a firm grip, then turned to
Bruce. "You've got a good mother. Listen to her."

The ride home was silent. Tess glanced toward
Bruce a couple of times, but in the dim light she
couldn't read his expression. Had tonight had any im-

pact at all? she wondered. Would it be a turning point—or only make things worse? Had she handled the situation the right way—or only widened the gulf between them? Unfortunately, Tess didn't have the answers to those questions, she acknowledged, deeply discouraged and suddenly bone weary as she pulled into a parking place near their apartment.

Bruce followed her to the door, head down, hands in his pockets. But she saw him take a deep breath when they stepped inside, heard his relieved sigh, could feel the almost palpable easing of tension. Tess dropped her purse on the couch and turned to him. "Are you hungry?"

He looked at her in surprise, his gaze wary. "Yeah."

"How about an omelet?"

"Okay."

"Why don't you go change while I make it?"

He didn't need any urging to shed the clothes he'd worn in jail, Tess noted. In fact, a moment later she also heard the shower running. Maybe his visit to the police station *had* made an impact, she thought hopefully.

She joined him at the table, sipping a white soda as he devoured the food.

"Aren't you going to eat anything?" he asked between bites.

She shook her head. The thought of food made her stomach even more queasy than it already was. "I had something at the carnival."

"With Mr. Jackson?"

"Yes."

He thought about that for a minute. "Are you going to tell him about this?"

"He won't need me to tell him. The police let the school know when any of the students get into trouble."

Bruce looked at her. "How do you know?"

"Mr. Jackson told me during the interview for the story."

"Is that legal?"

She almost laughed. "I think it's an informal thing, Bruce. Not an official report. Mr. Jackson used to be a cop, remember. He's got contacts there. They talk. Things come up."

"Yeah." His face fell. "He'll really be on me now."

Tess reached over and touched his hand. He seemed surprised, but he didn't pull away. "He cares about his students, Bruce. And I care about *you*. Can you imagine how frantic I was tonight when you didn't show up? And when the police called...." She choked and paused, struggling for control. "That's every parent's worse nightmare."

Bruce looked at her, the contrition in his eyes sincere. "I'm sorry, Mom," he said softly. "I didn't mean to worry you." He patted her hand awkwardly.

She looked at her son, tall now, the soft features of childhood giving way to the angular lines of adolescence. Lately she could see in his face the man he would soon become. Where had the years gone? she wondered in disbelief. It seemed like only yesterday that he was climbing onto her lap for a bedtime story. So much had changed in the intervening years, she thought wistfully.

But one thing hadn't changed. She still wished for him exactly what she had as she held him so tenderly in her arms the day he was born—a full and happy life, filled with love and satisfaction and contentment and a deep, abiding faith that would see him through adversity. She had vowed that day to do everything in her power to make that wish come true, and she had tried mightily through the years to honor that vow. That was why these past few weeks had been so difficult, she realized. They had reminded her that even deep maternal love couldn't shelter a child from the pain of loss or the consequences of mistakes. But she *could* stand by him. She *would* stand by him. And he needed to know that. To believe it.

"I know you didn't, Bruce. And I know you're going through a tough adjustment right now. I just wish I could put a bandage on the situation and make it better, like I did when you used to fall and scrape your knee. But I can't. You're old enough now to make a lot of your own decisions. All I can do is let you know that I'm always here for you. And that no matter what happens, I'll always love you. Will you remember that?"

Bruce nodded. "Yeah. And…I love you, too, Mom." Embarrassed now, he pushed his chair back and stood. "I guess I'll head to bed."

"Me, too." She stood as well and reached for him, closing her eyes against the world as she held him tightly for a long moment in a bear hug. "Sleep tight."

It was what she used to say as she tucked him in at night, and Bruce finished it for her. "And don't let the bedbugs bite."

"Things will be okay, Bruce," she told him fiercely, pulling back to look up at him. "Tomorrow can be a new beginning."

His eyes clouded, and the troubled expression he'd worn for the past few weeks slipped back into place. "Maybe," he replied noncommittally. "Good night, Mom."

Tess watched him disappear down the hall, tension coiling in her stomach once again. "Maybe" wasn't good enough. She wanted guarantees. But as she'd learned long ago, life didn't come with them.

Tess frowned, then highlighted the last few sentences in the article she'd written about Mitch and hit Delete. The closing was way too subjective. For the first time in her career she was having a hard time keeping her personal feelings out of her writing. And she was having lots of personal feelings. Too many, in fact. They kept intruding on her thoughts no matter how hard she tried to keep them at bay. And she was really trying. But it was a losing battle, she admitted with a resigned sigh.

The phone rang, and she reached for it distractedly, her gaze still on the screen.

"Tess Lockwood."

"Tess? It's Mitch. I heard about what happened Saturday night, and I just wanted to call and make sure everything was okay."

Tess's heart began to beat double time as the familiar, husky voice came over the wire. Suddenly it was no problem to transfer her attention from the screen to the phone.

"Hi." She berated herself for the sudden breathless

quality of her voice, praying he wouldn't notice. "Your timing is impeccable. I'm working on your story."

"Then you can probably use a break from the boredom."

She heard the self-deprecating humor in his voice and smiled. "Don't sell yourself short."

"Hey, I'm just a guy doing his job. Nothing more. But tell me about Saturday," he prompted, diverting the attention from himself. "I saw Bruce earlier today, and he seemed to have survived. What about you. Are you okay?"

Tess felt her throat tighten with emotion. Which was silly, of course. The call was nothing more than a follow-up with the mother of a problem student. But she was touched nonetheless.

"I'm fine," she replied. "And thank you for checking. I'm sure you're busy enough just keeping up with the students, let alone their parents. But that's probably why you're so good at what you do—and why you win awards."

Mitch frowned. Tess had assumed his call was professional. But was it? He hadn't stopped to analyze his motives when he'd decided to contact her. All he knew was that he wanted to reassure himself that Saturday's trauma hadn't rattled her too badly. But he knew that Tess was a strong woman. She didn't need him to check up on her. Yet he'd made the call anyway. Which led him to believe that it was motivated by reasons that had nothing to do with his job. And to let her think otherwise wasn't honest.

"Actually, I'm not always this good about follow-up with parents," he admitted.

There was silence on the other end of the line for a moment while Tess digested that comment. Was he implying a personal interest? Or just letting her know that Bruce's case needed more intervention and involvement than most? Tess had no idea. So she played it safe and stayed neutral.

"Then I especially appreciate the call. It's nice to know I'm not in this thing with Bruce completely alone."

Mitch's frown deepened. Did her polite, impersonal remark imply that she wanted to keep their relationship on a professional basis? Or was she still just running scared? Connected only by voice, with none of the visual cues he'd had at the carnival, Mitch was uncertain. And frustrated. Unfortunately, a phone conversation was not the way to get clarity. Which he would be wise not to seek anyway, he reminded himself firmly. Relationships had been off his radar screen for seven years. And it would be best if they stayed that way.

"Well, if I can help in any way, don't hesitate to call," he said, matching her impersonal, polite tone.

"I won't. And Mitch...thank you again."

The sudden warmth in her voice washed over him like a tropical wave, and his own voice heated up in response. "You're welcome. Goodbye, Tess."

As Tess slowly replaced the receiver and turned regretfully back to her computer, she realized that Caroline was standing in the doorway, grinning.

"I take it the interview went well."

Tess felt hot color steal over her cheeks. "How did you know?"

"I assume that was Mitch Jackson on the phone. I

only caught the tail end of the conversation, but from your tone of voice I gather you two clicked.''

"He was very...nice,'' Tess conceded self-consciously. ''I should have the story wrapped up before the end of the day.''

Caroline folded her arms across her chest and leaned against the edge of the cubicle wall. ''Is that all I'm going to get?'' she teased, her eyes twinkling.

Tess's flush deepened. ''There isn't any more to tell.''

"Hmm.'' Caroline studied her for a moment. ''So why did he call?''

"I had some trouble with Bruce Saturday night. He heard about it and wondered if everything was okay.''

Caroline frowned and straightened. ''Is it?''

Tess nodded. ''For the moment.'' She gave her boss a quick recap of the evening's events, then sighed. ''These last few weeks have really been a challenge. I'm lucky Mitch Jackson has taken such an interest.''

Caroline eyed her speculatively. ''I know he's committed to his work, or he wouldn't be winning awards,'' she conceded. ''But I doubt he makes a habit of checking to see how the parents of his students are doing. Unless his interest is more than academic.''

Tess stared after Caroline as her boss turned and disappeared around the corner. She wasn't sure the managing editor was right. But the possibility sent a tingle down her spine. However, her priority was Bruce. Period. Getting his life turned around would require every bit of her energy and attention.

With an effort Tess forced her attention back to the

words on the screen. Recalled something Mitch had
just said in their conversation. And suddenly had the
ending to her story.

"I'm just a guy doing his job. Nothing more," Tess
typed, attributing the quote to Mitch. Then she continued. "Clearly, the governor's office doesn't agree.
Mitch Jackson isn't just a man doing his job. He's a
man with a mission—doing a great job. And Southfield High is a better place because of it."

Tess leaned back. Mitch *was* a man with a mission.
Because he cared so much about the kids, he did his
job with focus, commitment and passion.

And suddenly Tess couldn't help but wonder what
it would be like if Mitch devoted that same focus,
commitment and passion to some lucky woman.

The answer came immediately to mind. And it was
all contained in one word.

Heaven.


Uncle Ray finished the article, took off his glasses
and carefully lowered the newspaper to the kitchen
table. "That's a mighty fine story, son. I'm proud of
you."

Mitch felt his neck grow hot. "Thanks, Uncle Ray.
I thought you'd like to see it. But frankly, I'm a little
embarrassed about the whole thing. I didn't get into
this line of work to be in the limelight."

"I know that. And I think it came through real clear
in the story. The reporter…" He picked up the paper
again and looked for the byline. "Tess Lockwood.
She sure seems to have caught your personality. And
all in one interview, too."

Mitch wrapped his hands around his coffee cup.

"Actually, we'd met before that. You remember the woman I mentioned when I was out here a few weekends ago? The one who's the mother of one of my problem students?"

Uncle Ray nodded. "I seem to recall something like that."

"Well, she works for the community newspaper. She did the story."

"Is that so?"

Mitch saw the sudden gleam in his uncle's eyes and held up his hand. "Don't jump to any conclusions, Uncle Ray. All of our meetings have been strictly professional."

The older man nodded sagely. "I'm sure they have. How is the boy doing, by the way?"

Mitch frowned. "Everything's been quiet for the past week. But there was an incident last weekend." He explained the car accident to the older man, who shook his head.

"Sounds like that boy needs a good talking-to."

"He does. Te…his mother is doing her best, but I think she may be in over her head on this one. Fourteen is a tough age, especially without a father figure. Bruce seems like a good kid, but he's in with the wrong crowd. Things worked out okay last weekend, but next time he may not be so lucky. I'm intervening where I can, but there's only so much I can do. I only see him during school hours. And even then, I doubt I'm having much impact. To him, I am definitely the enemy with a capital *E*."

"Hmm. That is a problem. Especially if you've taken a particular interest in this boy." Uncle Ray reached for his mug and took a sip of coffee. "You know, you might have more luck getting through to him if you could get him one-on-one outside of school. Let him see you in a different light. Might help him to see you more as a friend than an enemy.''

Mitch considered that. ''You could be right,'' he agreed.

''Why don't you invite him to come down here to the farm with you for Easter?''

Mitch stared at his uncle. ''Are you serious?''

The older man shrugged. ''Why not? Plenty of room. And the fresh air might do him some good.''

Now that the initial shock was wearing off, Mitch began to warm to the idea. ''You know, that just might work,'' he said slowly. ''His mother told me that when they lived in Jeff City, Bruce used to love visiting the farm of some friends of theirs.''

''There you go.''

Mitch regarded his uncle silently for a moment. ''I think you might be on to something, Uncle Ray. But what made you think of this? I've had lots of problem students through the years, and you've never suggested anything like this before.''

He shrugged. ''Can't say. Just seems like you've taken a special interest in this boy. And it sounds like he could be at a crossroads. I sort of fancy helping you help him pick the right route. Do you think his mother would agree to this?''

Mitch nodded. ''She wants to do whatever's best for her son.'' Then he frowned. ''But I hate to take him away from her on a holiday weekend. They only have each other, so she'd be alone.''

''Well, bring her along.''

Mitch stared at the older man. His uncle was full of surprises tonight. "Bring her along?"

"Sure. Like I said, plenty of room. Be nice to have the house full of people on a holiday for once."

While Uncle Ray was kind and generous to a fault and such a gesture was characteristic of him, there was something more going on here than mere philanthropy, Mitch deduced. Like maybe a bit of matchmaking. He took a sip of his coffee and carefully set it on the table.

"Uncle Ray, you wouldn't by any chance be trying to play Cupid here, would you?"

The older man could have won an Academy Award for the innocent look he gave his nephew. "Cupid? I think I'm a little old for that, don't you?"

Mitch grinned. "You're not too old for anything."

The hint of a smile touched Uncle Ray's lips. "How about some more coffee?" Without waiting for a response, he rose and walked over to the counter to retrieve the pot.

"You're avoiding the question," Mitch accused.

Uncle Ray looked over his shoulder and eyed his nephew shrewdly. "How did it come up, anyway? One minute I'm trying to be a good Christian by opening my home to a troubled youngster, and the next you're thinking about romance. And you think *I'm* the one who's got Cupid on my mind?"

Mitch frowned at his uncle's back. Somehow this conversation had gotten all turned around. Had he overreacted to Uncle Ray's generosity, read too much into it? Was he the one with cupid on his mind?

If he was honest, Mitch knew that the answers to those questions were *probably* and *definitely*. He couldn't deny that there was something about Tess Lockwood that had gotten under his skin. Or that she was invading his thoughts—and his heart—more and more. But why? And what was he going to do about it?

Uncle Ray had very adeptly avoided answering his question about Cupid, Mitch realized as the older man refilled his cup. But it didn't matter now. Because the questions he'd just asked himself were much more important, though the answers were just as elusive.

# Chapter Six

"This is a really dumb idea. Why can't we just stay home for Easter?"

Tess looked up as her son entered the living room and unenthusiastically dumped his duffel bag next to the couch. "Did you pack something nice for church on Sunday?"

"Do I have to go?"

"It's Easter."

"Big deal."

"Yes, it is," Tess replied firmly. "We've never missed church on Easter. The only reason we don't go every week now is because of my work schedule. But I miss it. A lot."

"I don't," Bruce shot back. "It's boring." He slouched into a chair, stretched out his long legs and scowled. "Why did you say yes to this, anyway?" he groused. "Three days with an ex-cop principal and an old man—some holiday."

Tess counted to ten—slowly—as she walked down

the hall to retrieve her suitcase. When she reached the sanctuary of her room, she took a deep breath and sat on the edge of the bed. She hadn't answered Bruce's question. Mostly because she didn't know the answer. The invitation had come out of the blue, taking her by surprise. And Mitch had said all the right things when he'd issued it. Things that made it hard to turn down. Like how beneficial it could be to his relationship with Bruce to let the boy see him in a different setting. And how good it might be for Bruce to get back to the country environment he'd once enjoyed so much, in simpler days. The rationale had seemed to make a lot of sense at the time. She was desperate to help Bruce, and Mitch had positioned this weekend in a way that made it sound almost therapeutic.

But that wasn't the only reason she'd accepted, Tess admitted. Yes, she was touched by Mitch's willingness to go the extra mile for Bruce. And yes, she believed that Mitch was sincerely convinced that a weekend in the country might be good for Bruce. But though Mitch was a dedicated principal who went above and beyond for his students, she really didn't think he invited most of them—and their mothers— to spend a holiday at his uncle's farm. Which meant that maybe, just maybe, part of his reason for asking was that he wanted to spend time with her. And even with her teenage son and his elderly uncle as chaperons, that thought sent a shiver of excitement through her.

Tess knew she wasn't being wise. After all, romance was *not* among her priorities. Her roles were clear and straightforward—mother and breadwinner. Period.

But in her heart she knew it wasn't quite that simple. Because she was a woman, too. And that part of her, those needs, had been suppressed far too long. Which hadn't been much of a problem, frankly, until Mitch came along. He made her feel like a desirable woman again, whether that was his intent or not. She had no idea of the depth of his interest in her, only that it had to be there, at some level, or this invitation would never have come.

Tess knew she shouldn't get carried away with romantic fantasies. But for just one weekend the temptation had been too great to resist. And what harm could it do? Bruce might very well benefit from the trip. As for her, a weekend with Mitch might help satisfy the longing in her soul for male companionship, even if only temporarily. It seemed to be a win-win situation all around. *If* she could get Bruce to cooperate, she reminded herself with a sigh as she hefted her suitcase.

The doorbell rang just as she reached the living room, sending her heart jumping to her throat. She glanced at her son, hoping he would buy her a moment to compose herself by answering the door, but he clearly had no intention of budging from the couch. She took a deep breath, willing the uncomfortable hammering of her heart to subside, but her body just wasn't cooperating, she realized helplessly.

A second ring from the bell and Bruce's curious look finally compelled her into action. She wiped her palms on her jeans and made her way to the door, praying for a modicum of composure. *Please, Lord, just let me get through the first few moments,* she pleaded. *Let me look cool and composed and in con-*

*trol. Let something clever and witty trip from my
tongue.*

But that was not to be. Because when she opened
the door and caught her first sight of Mitch, her pulse
went off the scale and her voice deserted her.

He was dressed more casually than she'd ever seen
him, in well-worn jeans and a forest-green shirt that
hugged his muscular chest and broad shoulders. His
dark hair was slightly windblown, and despite a slight
chill in the air, he exuded warmth. As Caroline had
noted, he was one handsome man.

But it was actually his smile that did her in. Compelling. Engaging. Intimate. It somehow seemed to
reach deep inside her, to a place no one had touched
for a long, long time. Her breath caught in her throat,
and the greeting she'd finally mustered died on her
lips.

For a moment their gazes connected and sizzled in
silence. When Mitch finally spoke, the husky quality
of his voice made her knees go weak, and her grip
on the door involuntarily tightened. "Good morning,
Tess."

"Hi." Her voice cracked, and she wanted to sink
through the floor. So much for being cool and witty.
She sounded like some schoolgirl with a crush on the
principal—and would probably be taken just about as
seriously, she thought, her spirits drooping. Mitch was
far too worldly to be interested in someone who acted
more like a lovesick student than a desirable woman.
And even if she wasn't in the market, it would be
nice to have someone look at her, just once, with fire
in his eyes. The smile on her lips suddenly felt stiff,
but she struggled to keep it in place.

Mitch could feel the tension in the air. The catch in her voice communicated her nervousness, and he didn't doubt that she'd had second thoughts about this weekend—just as he had. But now that he stood just inches away from her, any lingering doubts vanished. He not only *wanted* to spend time with this woman, he *needed* to, because at some very basic level he was drawn to her. Not just because she was beautiful, though he certainly appreciated her physical attributes. His gaze flickered over her quickly, discreetly, but his keen eyes missed nothing. Long, shapely legs eased into worn jeans that fit like a second skin. A waistline that seemed small enough for his hands to span. A soft, pink cotton shirt, open at the neck, that subtly molded her curves and revealed the pulse beating rapidly in the hollow of her throat. She was scared, nervous, uncertain…attracted?

He felt his own pulse accelerate as his gaze moved swiftly back to her eyes, past soft, slightly parted lips that seemed made to be kissed. And suddenly he was the one who was nervous.

"W-would you like to come in?" She stepped aside, and Mitch crossed the threshold, taking his time—and a long, slow breath—as he scanned the small but cozy room. Tess had done a good job with the apartment, he realized, noting the homey touches throughout. It was a friendly, welcoming place—except for the expression on Bruce's face, Mitch amended as his gaze connected with his problem student.

Mitch steadily returned the young man's hostile glare. This was the one part of the weekend he was *not* looking forward to. Getting through to Bruce, trying to put their relationship on a different footing, wasn't going to be easy. But it was important. Bruce was on the edge, and unless someone pulled him back soon, he could end up like...

As always, Mitch's gut clenched painfully, and he blocked out that image. He wasn't going to go there. Not today. But he was going to do everything in his power to keep Bruce from making the same mistakes. Just as he had for every troubled student who'd come his way ever since that night.

Despite the teenager's antagonistic look, Mitch smiled. "Hello, Bruce."

Bruce waited a long moment before mumbling a barely audible "Hi." Then he turned his attention back to the TV, pointedly ignoring the two adults by the door.

Tess frowned, but Mitch's smile was reassuring. "Everything will be fine," he said softly.

She gave him a worried look and spoke in a low voice. "I hope so. Bruce hasn't exactly been enthusiastic about this. I don't want him to ruin your holiday weekend."

"He won't."

She sighed. "I wish I could be so sure."

"Trust me on this."

She tilted her head and looked at him quizzically. "Do you know something I don't?"

Actually, he did. But he couldn't very well tell her that as long as she shared his holiday it was bound to be a good one. "Let's just say I'm an optimist," he offered. "And that I don't intend to let anything ruin this weekend."

Tess gave him a weary smile. "I like your attitude."

"It beats the alternative," he replied with a grin. "So are you ready? It's too pretty a day to waste in the city." He reached for her bag.

"We're all set. Bruce, help Mitch take the bags out to the car while I get the food."

Though Mitch had protested that it wasn't necessary, she'd insisted on contributing her homemade lasagna and cinnamon streusel coffee cake to the weekend's festivities. As she headed to the kitchen she glanced again toward Bruce, who was still slouched in front of the TV. "Now, Bruce," she said pointedly in a tone that brooked no argument.

By the time she returned from the kitchen, there was no sign of Bruce. She gave Mitch a quizzical look as he reached over to take the cooler of goodies.

"He's in the car," he replied to her silent question.

"Did he say anything?" Hope and fear mingled in her voice.

"No. But he'll loosen up."

She sighed. "I don't know. He's gotten pretty good at shutting people out."

At the pain and discouragement in her voice, Mitch felt his throat contract with emotion. Parenting an adolescent was never easy, even for two people. Doing it single-handedly while coping with a new job, a new town and a son having difficulty adapting to a new school made it even tougher. He knew that Tess was doing her best, and he was tempted to reassure her that things would work out. But he couldn't guarantee that. And he'd learned a long time ago not to make promises he couldn't keep.

"Maybe the change of scene will give him a new perspective," Mitch said encouragingly. "If nothing else, it will brighten up my uncle's holiday. He's really been looking forward to this. He doesn't have much company these days."

"I still can't believe he was willing to invite two total strangers to stay with him," Tess said, shaking her head. "He must be a very generous man. Will you tell me about him on the drive?"

"Sure."

By the time they pulled into the gravel drive leading to the modest, two-story frame farmhouse that Uncle Ray had called home for forty-five years, she'd learned a lot about the older man. His beloved wife had died eight years before, and his only son had been killed in Vietnam. Though his uncle had coped with those losses, relying on a deep-seated faith to see him through, Mitch confided that he often worried about the older man spending so much time alone. Yet his uncle never complained, saying that he was too busy to get lonely.

"Uncle Ray really is amazing," Mitch told her, the admiration clear in his voice. "Even though he's spent his life on a farm—and trust me, no one knows more than he does about corn and wheat and soybeans and soil and weather…you get the idea—his interests go far beyond the world of farming. And he's a voracious reader."

According to Mitch, he fancied biographies and, interestingly enough, romance novels, citing their optimism and happy endings as tonic for the soul in a world where the concept of lifelong love and commitment had somehow lost favor. Tess liked him already.

She'd also learned a lot about Mitch during their hour-long drive. It was clear that he felt a deep sense of responsibility toward his uncle—more, perhaps, than required by mere kinship. She sensed that these two men shared some sort of special bond, though Mitch revealed nothing that would verify that hunch. When he spoke of his uncle his voice held unmistakable affection, and if he ever resented spending his rare free time working with the older man on the farm, he gave no indication of it. Generosity, it appeared, ran in the Jackson family.

Tess glanced into the back seat a couple of times during the drive, hoping to pull Bruce into the conversation, but he was hunched into the corner, his eyes closed. He might be sleeping, but more likely he was simply making a statement that he had no intention of participating in this weekend, she speculated resignedly.

"There's Uncle Ray."

Tess transferred her gaze to the house at the end of the gravel drive they'd just turned into, where an older man stood on the porch, waiting to greet them. Tall and spare, with fine, neatly trimmed gray hair, he radiated strength and tenacity—as if he had weathered the storms of life much as the huge oak tree in his front yard had weathered the storms of nature.

As they pulled to a stop by the front porch, he made his way a bit stiffly down the three steps. During the drive Mitch had told her more about the accident that had predicated his own move to St. Louis, and she could now see firsthand the lingering effects of it. She knew it must be difficult for Mitch's uncle, an independent man who was used to doing things on his own, to have to rely on help from others to keep up with the farm.

Mitch set the parking brake and smiled at her. "Welcome to my home away from home. Sit tight and I'll get your door."

She didn't protest, waiting as the two men shared an uninhibited bear hug as they met in front of the car. She caught a glimpse of Bruce in the visor mirror and saw that he was awake—and watching the exchange. Good. Seeing Mitch in this caring context, relaxed and removed from his official capacity, was exactly what Bruce needed. Maybe in this environment he would realize that the principal truly had his best interests at heart, that his concern was genuine. And then maybe…just maybe…he would allow Mitch to get close enough to give him some guidance. Tess prayed that would happen soon. Because she knew that she desperately needed help with her son, just as she intuitively knew that Mitch could provide it.

A moment later Mitch opened her door and reached down to take her hand, drawing her toward his uncle.

"Uncle Ray, I'd like you to meet Tess Lockwood. Tess, this is my uncle."

He released her hand, and Uncle Ray engulfed her slender fingers in a work-worn grip. His voice was warm and welcoming when he spoke, and his cobalt-blue eyes were kindly—and as sharp and insightful as those of his nephew. "It's a pleasure to meet you, Tess. Mitch has told me quite a lot about you, and I've been looking forward to this weekend."

She mulled over that nugget of information as she returned his greeting, trying to focus on the older man's words rather than the delicious memory of Mitch's hand momentarily holding hers. What exactly had Mitch told his uncle? Nothing bad, obviously, because the man appeared to be genuinely glad to make her acquaintance. In fact, more than glad. There was a gleam of interest in his eye that somehow seemed to go beyond mere hospitality. But before she could analyze it, he'd turned his attention to Bruce, who had gotten out of the car and now stood somewhat awkwardly behind the adults.

"And you must be Bruce. Mitch tells me you're new at school this semester. Must be hard, makin' that kind of transition in the middle of the year. Never did like changes, myself. But the good Lord just keeps dishin' 'em out. That's life, I expect, whether you're a senior in high school or a senior citizen like me. Hope you like farms."

Bruce seemed somewhat taken aback by the older man's lengthy greeting. "Uh, yeah. I do."

"Good. I'll show you around later. But first, let's get everybody settled."

Tess found herself in the guest room, while Bruce was given the room once occupied by Uncle Ray's son. The older man planned to give Mitch his room, but his nephew insisted on taking the couch in the den.

Once they were all settled, they regrouped in the cheery country kitchen for lunch.

"I hope this is all right," Uncle Ray said anxiously as he passed around the plates. "I'm not much versed in entertaining. That was always my wife's department, and since she passed on eight years ago, I haven't had many people over. 'Cept Mitch, of course. He's a regular. Best farmhand I ever had, matter of fact. And not too picky when it comes to eating. Good thing, too. My repertoire is limited. That's why I got some fancy store-bought food for lunch. I heard city folks like quiche.''

''Don't let him fool you,'' Mitch warned, his eyes twinkling. ''He makes a mean meat loaf. And the best beef stew I've ever tasted.''

''Can't take any credit for those,'' Uncle Ray said as he eased himself into a chair at the head of the polished wooden table. ''After Emma passed on, I got to craving some of her specialties, so I dug up her old cookbooks. Took some practice, but I finally mastered a few. Matter of fact, we're having one of my favorites tonight. Tuna casserole. Nothing fancy, but real tasty.''

''Bruce is a great fan of tuna anything,'' Tess told him.

''Well, then I picked the right thing, I guess,'' the older man said. ''I've been partial to it myself since I was a teenager. How old are you, son?''

''Fourteen.''

''Is that right? I would have guessed sixteen.''

That seemed to please Bruce. ''I'm tall for my age.''

''I'd say so. Probably top six feet by the time you stop growing. Why, you might even pass Mitch.''

That seemed to please him even more. ''I'd like to be tall.''

''Why is that?''

Bruce shrugged. "People can't push you around as much if you're bigger than they are."

Uncle Ray nodded thoughtfully. "I suppose that's true. Course, bein' tall isn't the only way to get respect. There was a man lived down the road a piece when I was younger. Couldn't have been more than five-five, five-six. And nobody ever pushed him around. Looked up to him, in fact."

Bruce polished off the last bite of his quiche and looked at Uncle Ray with interest. "Why?"

"I suppose it was because he always did the right thing. And I mean *always*. Not to mention the fact that he lived by the golden rule. Never turned anybody away who was in need, and was always the first to help in times of trouble. Amazing thing, too, considering a lot of the people he helped weren't so nice to him when he was young. Called him 'shorty' and 'stubs' and lots of other things, from what I hear. Treated him pretty bad, sort of like an outcast." Uncle Ray shook his head. "Kids can be real mean sometimes."

Out of the corner of her eye Tess saw Bruce's nod of affirmation.

"But he never let it turn him bitter or spiteful or mean. He just went about his business, doing his best. Never gave anyone a lick of trouble, though I expect if he'd wanted to get even with some of the kids who were giving him a hard time, there were opportunities. But eventually all those boys grew up, and then they recognized what a fine person Roger was. The girls did, too, by the way. In fact, Roger married the prettiest girl in town and raised three fine sons. He passed on to his reward twenty, twenty-five years ago now, but nobody who ever met him forgot him. And you know, when I think of him now, I remember him as one of the tallest men I ever knew.''

Bruce pondered that for a few moments. ''It wasn't fair, what those guys did to him when he was young. He couldn't help being short.''

''That's a fact,'' Uncle Ray agreed.

Mitch's uncle had hit on a theme that was near and dear to Bruce's heart. How many times had she heard the sometimes plaintive, sometimes bitter expression ''But it's not fair'' in the past few months? More than she could count. And considering the frown on her son's face right now, he was wrestling with the concept yet again. She wished she'd been able to come up with an explanation for the vagaries of the world, but in her heart she knew there wasn't one. Bottom line, that was just how life worked. So maybe Uncle Ray's response was best. Just acknowledge it rather than try to explain it. Bruce seemed to respect that.

''How about a tour of the farm, Uncle Ray?''

Mitch's voice broke the brief silence, and she smiled at the older man. ''Yes, that would be lovely.''

''Mitch knows the place as well as I do. Why don't you two go on and we'll catch up with you? Me and Bruce are gonna have some more of that fancy quiche. What do you say, Bruce? It's pretty good for store-bought stuff.''

''Yes, sir.''

Tess stared at her son. She hadn't heard him call anyone ''sir'' in—well, not since they'd moved to St. Louis. Amazing.

Tess studied the older man as he rose to cut two more slices of quiche. He'd given little indication since their arrival that he knew the extent of Bruce's problems. But Tess expected that Mitch had filled him in pretty thoroughly. And she also suspected that the casual conversation about fairness and respect might have been carefully orchestrated by Uncle Ray. Which impressed her.

But what impressed her even more was that Bruce was listening. For some reason, he seemed to have connected with Mitch's uncle. That wasn't exactly what she'd expected this weekend—nor hoped for, if she was honest—but if Bruce bonded with Uncle Ray rather than Mitch, so be it. As long as it helped him get his act together, she was all for it.

Uncle Ray returned to the table with two more loaded plates, and as Bruce began to ply the man with questions about the farm, Mitch grinned at Tess. ''I don't think we'll be missed here. How about that tour?''

''Sounds good.''

As they stood, Uncle Ray looked up at them. ''You two take your time. Bruce and I have plenty to talk about.''

Tess gave Mitch a ''Do you believe this?'' look and followed him outside. Neither spoke until the door was firmly closed behind them, at which point Mitch voiced her exact thoughts.

''I see signs of progress already.''

Tess looked up at him. ''How in the world did your uncle do that?'' she asked wonderingly as they strolled toward the barn.

Mitch shook his head. ''If I knew that, I'd be ten times more successful with my students. He has an amazing ability to empathize with people. Young or old, rich or poor, man or woman, he has this uncanny knack of knowing exactly the right things to say to draw people out. And he listens well. I hadn't really thought about him and Bruce clicking, but something is going on in there, that's for sure. In fact, I feel a bit like the odd man out," he teased.

Tess smiled. "Hardly. If it wasn't for you, we'd be spending the holiday in a cramped apartment instead of this glorious place." She paused at the edge of a field and leaned on the fence. The freshly turned earth was rich and dark, and a pond shimmered in the distance. Puffy white clouds billowed lazily in the deep blue sky, and the silence was interrupted only by an occasional bird call or the distant moo of a cow. She closed her eyes and lifted her face to the sun, feeling the tension melt away from her. "This is the perfect antidote for a weary soul," she said with a sigh.

Mitch angled toward her and propped one arm on the fence. She looked at peace for the first time since he'd met her, he realized, as the bright, midday light turned the reddish highlights in her hair to glints of fire. The fine lines of strain around her eyes were dissolving under the caressing warmth of the sun, and he watched as she drew in a deep, cleansing breath. Since her eyes were still closed, he took the opportunity to let his gaze leisurely trace her upturned profile, drinking in the smooth brow, perfect nose, full lips, firm chin and the delicate, slender column of her throat. Her loveliness alone would attract any man, but coupled with what he already knew of her character, he couldn't help but think again what a fool her husband had been. Even if he'd married her for the wrong reasons, how could he have failed to eventually realize what a treasure he'd found? And how could he not love the son she'd borne out of their union? It boggled his mind.

And it made him angry. Very angry. Bruce's father had hurt his son in ways that Mitch could clearly discern. And in throwing away the love of the special woman who now stood beside him, her husband had hurt her in ways that Mitch could only begin to imagine. Ways he wished with all his heart he could erase.

Tess chose that moment to open her eyes, and the expression on Mitch's face made her heart stop, then race on. He was gazing at her with such intense tenderness that it took her breath away. No one had ever looked at her like that, as if she was someone precious to be cherished and protected. Her lips parted in surprise, and she unconsciously lifted her hand to her throat.

At her movement, Mitch very deliberately—and with obvious difficulty—altered his expression from tenderness to simple friendliness. She watched his Adam's apple bob convulsively, and his voice was noticeably husky when he spoke.

"We haven't made much progress on our tour. Come on, I'll show you the barn."

He took her arm as they traversed the uneven ground, and Tess hoped he wouldn't feel the tremors that ran through her. Maybe they hadn't seen much of the farm, but she'd learned a lot more than she'd bargained for a few moments ago, when she'd turned to him and caught his unguarded expression.

Tess wasn't very worldly. She hadn't had much experience with men other than her husband, and she'd been out of the dating game for a very long time. But she knew enough to recognize when a man was interested. And Mitch was definitely interested.

The question was, did he intend to pursue his interest? And if so, how was she going to handle it? Because unless he and Bruce established a truce, any involvement she had with the boy's enemy could make her son bond more closely with the gang that had become his adopted family. And that could only lead to disaster.

Tess's spirits took a nosedive. Her current dilemma confirmed what she already knew. Life was filled with difficult choices. And as Bruce had recently discovered, it often wasn't fair.

# Chapter Seven

"Hey, Uncle Ray, that ship-in-a-bottle is cool! Where did you get it?" Bruce handed the older man his glasses, which he'd volunteered to fetch from the bedroom, then sat beside him in front of the computer in the den.

Uncle Ray took the glasses and adjusted them on his nose as he turned on the computer. "My son, Jeff, made that for me many years ago."

"No kidding! How did he get all those big pieces in there?"

"With a great deal of patience and skill. He was good at that kind of thing. Would have made a fine surgeon, I think. That's what he wanted to be."

There was a momentary pause, and when Bruce spoke again his voice was tentative. "On the way down here I heard Mr. Jackson tell Mom that he got killed in Vietnam."

"That's right."

"You must have been real sad."

Uncle Ray took off his glasses and swiveled away from the computer to look directly at Bruce. He studied the boy for a moment, as if debating how to respond. "That's a fair statement, son. It's real hard when someone you love dies, especially when they're so young. And when it didn't have to be."

Bruce frowned. "What do you mean?"

Uncle Ray sighed and carefully set his glasses next to the computer. "I was once a very stubborn man, Bruce," he said quietly. "After I made up my mind about something, I couldn't see things any other way. That's how it was about that war. When I was growing up, young men went to war when they were called. Maybe they didn't like it, but they went anyway, because it was the right thing to do. But Jeff didn't see it that way. Not for that war, anyway. He didn't believe in what we were doing in Vietnam. In fact, he felt so strongly about it that he wanted to go to Canada to avoid the draft."

"Could he have done that?"

"Yes. Some young men did."

"Was that wrong?"

Uncle Ray gazed into the distance. "I thought so at the time. And I told Jeff so. Plus a lot of other things. I told him that he was being unpatriotic. That I'd always thought he had guts, but I wasn't so sure anymore. And that I was ashamed of him."

The answer was plain, straightforward and painfully honest, given without excuses and unsparing in its harshness. But the raw regret and deep sadness in the older man's voice eloquently communicated his anguish. Instinctively Bruce reached over and touched his arm.

Uncle Ray looked at Bruce and laid his work-worn fingers over the boy's hand. "I'm sure you can guess the rest, son. Jeff loved me so much he couldn't bear for me to be ashamed of him. So he put aside his own convictions and went when he was drafted. He was only over there two weeks when we got word he'd been killed in an ambush in the jungle."

Bruce's voice was hushed when he spoke. "I'm sorry, Uncle Ray."

The older man patted his hand. "Thank you, son. I am, too. I still miss Jeff every day, even after all these years. And I still regret that he never got to be that surgeon. Could have done a lot of good for a lot of people, I think. It was such a waste." He sighed and shook his head. "Took me a long time to learn to live with myself after that. Had a lot of conversations with the Lord about it. Didn't seem fair, him gone, me still here, when it was my mistake. 'Cause the fact is, I was wrong about that war."

Bruce looked at him curiously. "It's kind of weird to hear an adult admit they're wrong."

Uncle Ray smiled gently. "Let me tell you something, Bruce. Admitting mistakes, having the courage to say you're wrong, is a sign of growing up. Trouble is, a lot of people never learn to do that. Or they learn too late. Like me. I didn't get a second chance with my mistake. But lots of times people do, and if we're smart, the next time we do better."

"I guess everybody makes mistakes," Bruce said slowly, his brow creased with a frown.

"That's a fact. Important thing is to learn from them." Uncle Ray picked up his glasses and settled them back on his nose. "Okay, that's enough heavy stuff for today. Let's surf."

"Man, he is one cool dude."

Tess gave the spaghetti sauce one final stir and turned to Bruce. Instead of the perennial scowl he'd worn for the past few months, his face was animated and eager. Uncle Ray had certainly made an impression. Bruce had talked of little else since their visit to the farm a week before.

"What's the latest?"

Bruce straddled a kitchen chair. "He just sent me an e-mail about this great Web site he found on the Pilgrims, to help me with the research for my history paper. Did you know that they landed at Plymouth Rock because they ran out of beer?"

Tess chuckled. "Can't say that I did. Are you sure about that?"

"Yeah. The Web page has part of a journal from the ship, and it says they had to land because they ran out of food and stuff, especially beer. Mr. Landis knows a lot about history, but I bet he doesn't know that."

"You could be right."

Bruce rose and helped himself to some cookies from the jar on the counter.

"You know, Mom, Uncle Ray could use some help on the farm and I was thinking...well, I've got spring break coming up in two weeks, so I thought maybe...if he wanted me to...I could spend the week with him."

Tess looked at him in surprise. "Did he invite you?"

"No. Not exactly. Not yet. But I think he would, if I volunteered to help him."

Tess reached over to stir the spaghetti sauce again, buying herself a moment to think. A week on the farm was certainly preferable to a week with the group he'd been hanging around with at school. And Bruce and Uncle Ray had certainly seemed to hit it off. They'd been e-mailing daily. It was a completely unexpected turn of events, but Tess was nonetheless grateful. Bruce had seemed more like his old self ever since their visit to the farm, and she was willing to support anything that made a positive impact. But she wasn't willing to take advantage of the older man's generosity, even though the temptation was great.

"It would be okay with me, Bruce," she replied finally. "But Uncle Ray might not want two week-long house guests."

"Two?"

"Mitch will probably be there, too."

Bruce's face fell. "Yeah. I forgot about that."

"I'll tell you what. I'll ask Mitch to talk to Uncle Ray and see if he's willing to take on one more farmhand for the week."

Bruce frowned. "I don't know. When we were there for Easter, I kind of had Uncle Ray to myself. It wouldn't be the same this time."

"Maybe it would be better."

He gave her a look that said, "Get real."

"Why is that so unlikely?" she persisted. "You haven't had any trouble with Mitch at school lately."

"He's still the principal."

"He could also be your friend, if you'd let him."

"Like he's yours?"

The unexpected question, delivered in an accusatory tone, startled her. "What do you mean?"

Bruce shrugged stiffly. "You call him Mitch. And you two seemed real friendly at Uncle Ray's."

Tess felt hot color steal onto her cheeks, and she bent down on the pretense of looking for a lid in the cabinet. She'd tried to keep her growing feelings for Mitch in check, but apparently Bruce had picked up some undercurrents. Had Mitch, as well? The thought made her cheeks grow even warmer, and she rummaged even more vigorously in the cabinet. *Get a grip,* she admonished herself tersely. *You could be overreacting here. Play it cool.*

"Well, I guess we have become friends," she said, striving for a conversational tone as she straightened up. "He's a very nice man, Bruce."

"Yeah. Right."

Tess folded her arms and leaned back against the counter. "You may not want to believe that, Bruce, but it's true. He cares about people. Especially his students. He could be your friend if you let him."

"I have enough friends."

They were moving onto dangerous territory, and she didn't want to get into an argument that could propel him back into the arms of his so-called friends. Since Bruce had been grounded after the car accident, his contact with his "group" had been limited to school hours. Interestingly enough, he hadn't complained much. Nor had he talked about his brief visit to jail. Maybe she was being naive, but Tess had a feeling the events of that night had had a big impact. As had the trip to the farm. With things going so well, she didn't want to rock the boat. If Bruce didn't want to associate with Mitch, so be it.

"Have it your way," she said, trying for a nonchalant tone as she pushed away from the counter and turned back to the spaghetti sauce. "So should we forget about the farm for spring break?"

Tess held her breath while he mulled her question over in silence.

"I'll think about it," he finally said noncommittally as he snagged another cookie and headed toward his room.

Tess watched him disappear down the hall, her expression troubled. He hadn't said no outright. Which was a good sign, she told herself encouragingly.

What wasn't so good was his reaction to her relationship with Mitch. She'd felt him withdrawing as they discussed her "friendship" with the principal. And she couldn't let that happen. Bruce needed to think of her as an ally, not a traitor. So until he made peace with Mitch, she needed to keep her distance. Make that *if* he made peace with Mitch, she corrected herself.

Tess sighed. She'd known all along that her feelings for Mitch could get her into trouble. Especially since the attraction appeared to be mutual.

Then again, she could be wrong. She didn't have much experience in such things. And she hadn't heard from him once since their trip to the farm, though her heart had skipped a beat every time the phone rang. Maybe he had been interested, but the attraction had waned during their weekend at the farm. Or more likely she'd just read more into his kindness than was intended. Chalk it up to the overreaction of a lonely woman starved for affection, she thought with a bit-tersweet pang.

Besides, if Mitch *was* attracted to her, things could get really complicated. It was better this way.

At least for Bruce.

Bruce wasn't sure what had awakened him, but suddenly he was staring wide-eyed at the ceiling above him. Or at least in the direction of the ceiling. It was too dark to see anything. He turned and squinted at the illuminated dial of the clock on his nightstand. Two o'clock in the morning. That was weird. He never woke up in the middle of the night. Unless he was sick or something. But he felt fine.

With a shrug he flopped onto his back and closed his eyes. Better get back to sleep or he'd never make it through the American lit class tomorrow. Mrs. Be-derman's droning voice was a sure cure for insomnia, he thought with a sleepy grin, especially on Fridays. In fact, just last week Dan...

Suddenly his eyes flew open again. Now he knew what had awakened him. That low, moaning sound. From his mom's bedroom. Cold fear gripped him, and he swung his legs over the side of the bed and took off at a run.

He stopped in front of her door, which was un-characteristically shut, and knocked cautiously. "Mom?"

There was no response, but now he could hear the sound much more clearly. Something was really wrong. Without bothering to knock again, he pushed the door open. And that's when he got really scared.

Tess was lying on her side, doubled up, gasping for

breath. Her face was gray, her eyes were tightly closed and beads of sweat dotted her forehead.

"Mom?" He dropped down beside her and touched her shoulder, his voice laced with panic. "Mom?"

Her eyelids flickered open, and for a moment she seemed to have trouble focusing.

"Mom, what's wrong?"

Even through a fog of pain Tess could hear the fear in his voice. And though his face was hazy, the terror in his eyes was clear.

"I got sick…a couple of hours ago," she gasped. "I didn't want to…bother you, so I shut the door, but…the pain just keeps…getting worse."

Bruce's face drained of color. "What's wrong?"

"I…don't know." She closed her eyes again and moaned.

"What should I do?"

No response. Bruce wasn't sure if she'd even heard him. And if she had, she was too sick to give him any instructions.

Bruce stood and stared down at his mom. He'd seen her sick before. She'd had the flu last winter, in fact. But he'd never seen her like this. Something was really wrong. She needed help—fast.

Bruce ran to the kitchen, snatched up the phone and punched in 911. The woman on the other end took some preliminary information and assured him that an ambulance was on the way.

He raced back to Tess's room, where he dropped down beside her and awkwardly laid his hand on her shoulder. His heart was hammering so hard he thought it would burst through his chest at any moment. "It will be okay, Mom," he said, his voice quivering.

And for the first time in a long time he prayed.

The policeman laid his hand on Bruce's shoulder. "Is there someone you can call? A family member?"

Bruce watched the paramedics carry his mom out on a stretcher. He'd never felt so alone in his life. "We don't have any family. It's just me and my mom."

"How about a friend, then?"

A friend. He thought of the guys at school, and just as quickly dismissed them. They weren't the kind of people you called in an emergency. He thought of Uncle Ray. But the older man was a long way away. He needed somebody *now*. Somebody who would know what to do in an emergency like this. Somebody you could count on to take care of things. Somebody you could trust.

His gaze suddenly fell on Mitch Jackson's card, still thumbtacked to the message board in the kitchen. That was the *last* person he wanted to call.

But he knew with absolute certainty that Mitch Jackson was the *right* person to call.

Mitch didn't like middle-of-the-night phone calls. Never had. They almost always spelled trouble.

So when the phone rang at twenty minutes past two in the morning, he was instantly awake.

"Yes." His voice was clipped, terse.

Silence on the other end. He frowned, impatient now. "Hello?"

"Mr. Jackson? It—it's Bruce Lockwood."

The voice was high and tight, teetering on the edge of hysteria. He swung his feet over the side of his bed and reached for his shirt as a wave of fear coursed through him.

"Okay, Bruce, I'm here. Tell me what's wrong." It took every ounce of his self-control to modulate his voice, keep his own terror from showing.

A strangled sob. "My m-mom's sick. I called 911 and the paramedics are taking her to the hospital."

Mitch felt as if someone had kicked him in the gut. "Which hospital?"

Muffled voices while Bruce asked the policeman, then relayed the information to Mitch.

"That's a fine hospital, Bruce. They'll take good care of her. You ride with the paramedics, and I'll meet you there. Okay?"

"Yeah."

The line went dead. For a moment Mitch just sat there, numb. Tess seriously sick? It was inconceivable. She'd been fine at the farm. More than fine, in fact. Beautiful. Vivacious. And very, very desirable. That's why he'd kept his distance since their return, though he'd lost track of the number of times he'd been tempted to reach for the phone and dial her number. And now she was in an ambulance on her way to the hospital.

Another surge of adrenaline shot through him, and he went into action. Pants. Wallet. Socks. Where were his socks? Forget the socks. Shoes. He was in the car in three minutes flat.

Bruce was in the waiting room when he arrived, a forlorn figure huddled in a straight chair, who looked as scared as he'd sounded. For the first time in their relationship the boy actually seemed happy to see him.

Mitch strode toward him and instinctively placed a hand on his thin, trembling shoulder.

"You okay?" His voice was gentle.

"Yeah."

"Has anyone talked to you yet?"

"Only to ask about insurance."

Mitch bit back a curse. There was something wrong with a health-care system that would ask a scared kid about insurance in the middle of the night. "Okay. Sit tight. I'll find out how your mom is doing."

In five minutes Mitch had his answer. Appendicitis. They were running some tests to verify the preliminary diagnosis, but given the symptoms, the doctors were 99 percent sure. Their biggest concern was removing it before it ruptured. Tess had already authorized surgery, and they were prepping her now. They'd do laparoscopy if possible, to minimize postoperative pain and recovery, but they wouldn't know for sure if that was feasible until they got a look at the appendix.

Mitch relayed all this to Bruce when he rejoined him in the waiting room. He didn't minimize the problem, but neither did he make it sound like life or death.

"So will she be okay?" Bruce asked anxiously when Mitch finished.

"I'm sure she will," he replied honestly. "But depending on which kind of surgery they do, she could be pretty sore for a while. She'll need some help with day-to-day things."

"I can help her."

"I know you can."

Mitch didn't add that she'd need more help than a fourteen-year-old boy could provide. There would be time for that later. First they needed to get past the surgery.

They didn't talk much while they waited. Mitch got them both a soda at one point, but Bruce refused food. Mitch could understand that. His own stomach was roiling. Hospitals always did that to him. They simply sat there, together. And that was enough.

Three hours later, it was over. Fortunately the more minor, less invasive surgery had been possible. The doctor, still dressed in his surgical garb, told this to Bruce and Mitch just as the morning light was beginning to touch the horizon through the window.

"She'll be just fine," he assured them. "But she'll be sore for a few days. And she'll need to take it easy for a couple of weeks."

"When can she come home?" Bruce asked, the relief in his voice almost palpable.

"Probably tomorrow, if things go well. And I have no reason to think they won't."

"Can I see her?"

"She's in recovery right now, but she should be awake enough to talk to you in an hour or so." The doctor turned to Mitch, who had already identified himself as a friend. "I'll let the nurse know where to find you. And then I'd suggest you both go home and get some sleep," he added with a weary smile. "That's what I intend to do."

As the man departed, Bruce turned to Mitch. "What about school?"

"I'll call for both of us. After we see your mom,

I think we better follow the doctor's advice. I don't know about you, but four hours of sleep doesn't cut it for me.'' Actually, Mitch had survived on far less. But Bruce couldn't. And he wasn't about to leave the boy alone after his traumatic night.

"I am pretty beat," Bruce admitted.

"So how about some bacon and eggs while we wait for your mom to wake up?"

Bruce's eyes lit up. "Yeah! I'm starved."

Tess felt strange. As if she was floating. And she was cold. Really cold. So cold her teeth were chattering. Then someone tucked a nice warm blanket around her. She smiled and snuggled deeper under it. That felt good.

"Is she okay?"

Tess heard the voice. It sounded like Bruce.

Now a woman was speaking. "She's fine. Most patients are cold after surgery. The operating room is pretty chilly."

Surgery? Operating room? Was someone sick?

"Is she awake?"

Tess knew that voice, too. It had filled her dreams for the past few weeks. So this must be a dream, too.

"Half and half. But she'll be coming out of it pretty rapidly now."

Who on earth were they talking about? Tess wondered, struggling to open eyelids that felt heavy as lead. She tried to reach up, but someone restrained her hand, engulfing it in a warm, tender clasp.

"It's Mitch, Tess. And Bruce. Just rest. Don't try to move around. We're here with you."

The gentle voice sounded so real. Not like a dream

at all. This time her eyelids cooperated, and she stared up at the fuzzy world above her.

"Hi, Mom."

Bruce's voice. Her eyes sought out the source. She frowned, trying to focus. There were two faces above, and slowly the fuzzy images became clear.

"Bruce? Mitch?" Was that raspy voice hers?

"Welcome back."

She gazed up at Mitch. She'd never seen him look so—disheveled. He was sporting a day's growth of beard, his shirt was wrinkled, his hair was tousled and there were deep lines of worry and fatigue etched into his face. With a frown she turned to Bruce. He didn't look much better. His face was pale and his hair was sticking up in odd spikes. There was something very wrong here.

"Are you guys okay?" she rasped.

Mitch felt his throat tighten with tenderness. How like her to think first of them. He glanced at Bruce. "You've got quite a mom, you know that."

Bruce blinked rapidly and swiped at his eyes. "Yeah. I know."

Mitch bent down so that his eyes were only inches from Tess's. She stared into them, mesmerized by the glints of gold—and the tenderness—in their dark brown depths.

"We're fine, Tess. But you just had an emergency appendectomy."

The events of the night before suddenly came rushing back. The searing pain. The nausea. The disorienting ride in the ambulance.

"It was a relatively simple surgery," Mitch continued. "But not a moment too soon. If Bruce hadn't called the ambulance when he did, it could have been a very different story. The doctor said your appendix was on the verge of rupturing. Thanks to Bruce, they caught it in time."

Tess transferred her gaze to her son. She reached out to him, and he took her hand.

"Why am I not surprised?" she said softly. "I've always been able to count on him."

Bruce's face reddened. "Not so much lately," he amended, clearly struggling with the admission. "But I'll try to do better, Mom. I promise."

Tess's eyes filled with tears. If it had taken an evening in jail and appendicitis to make Bruce see the light, it was a small price to pay. "I believe you, Bruce. And I love you."

"I love you, too, Mom."

Mitch watched the exchange, encouraged that Bruce seemed to truly be on the road to a turn-around—and surprised by a sudden, sharp stab of jealousy. It took him all of two seconds to figure out his reaction. While they might look like a cozy little family group, the only family here was Tess and Bruce. Mitch was an outsider.

That hurt. A lot. And reminded him of what was missing from his life. It had been a long time since he'd thought about having a family. A long time since he'd *let* himself think about it. Because it just wasn't in the cards for him. He'd had his chance once. And blown it big time. Now he focused on helping kids. It was good work. Worthy work. Work that had made a difference in countless lives.

But it was also lonely work. Because when the families he worked with went home at night, they had each other. He had no one. Except Uncle Ray, of course. Thank God for Uncle Ray! But as kind and good as the older man was, he couldn't fill the empty place in Mitch's heart that was made for a wife and family.

"If these gentlemen will let go of your hands, I think it's time we got you settled in your room."

The teasing tone of the nurse jolted him back to reality, and he and Bruce simultaneously relinquished their hold on Tess. She missed their touch immediately.

The nurse smiled and gave her a wink. "Don't worry, it's only a temporary situation. I have a feeling these two handsome men aren't going to let you out of their sight for very long. They waited a long time for you to wake up."

Tess frowned. "What time is it?"

The nurse consulted her watch. "Seven o'clock."

"How long have you two been up?"

"Since about two o'clock," Bruce replied. "I called Mr. Jackson when the ambulance got there."

Tess looked at Mitch. "I want you both to go home and get some rest. And Mitch...I hate to ask, but could you call Caroline James at the newspaper for me? Let her know I won't be in?"

"No problem. And don't worry about Bruce. He can stay at my place till you're released."

The two Lockwoods stared at him, one in gratitude, the other in shock.

"Mom, I can stay by myself. Honest," Bruce spoke up quickly. "The doctor says you can probably come home tomorrow. I'll be fine till then."

Tess reached out to take his hand again. "I won't

get any rest if I'm worrying about you all by yourself in the apartment. Stay with Mitch. For me.''

Put that way, it was pretty hard to refuse. But Bruce was clearly not happy about the turn of events. ''I guess it will be okay for one night,'' he acquiesced reluctantly.

Tess smiled and squeezed his hand. ''Thank you.'' Then she turned to Mitch and, without even thinking about it, reached for his hand, as well. He laced his fingers with hers in a reassuring touch that communicated both caring and rock-solid strength. ''And thank *you*.''

Their gazes met briefly, but it was long enough for Tess to know one thing with absolute certainty.

The attraction *was* mutual.

# *Chapter Eight*

Mitch reached down for Bruce's duffel bag, then paused as a half-hidden stack of canvases in the boy's bedroom caught his eye. He squatted down to examine the top one, a pastoral fall landscape vibrant with color and life. The room grew still, and Mitch sensed Bruce moving behind him.

Mitch studied the impressive canvas silently for a long moment, then turned slowly. "Did you paint this?"

A flush seeped onto the teenager's face and he shoved his hands into his pockets. "Yeah. It's not very good."

Mitch looked again at the canvas, then nodded to the stack. "May I?"

Bruce shrugged indifferently, but stayed close as Mitch carefully examined each painting. By the time Mitch reached the last one he was completely blown away by the boy's talent. Once more he turned and looked up at Bruce.

"These are incredible."

The boy's flush deepened at the straightforward, sincere compliment. "They're okay, I guess."

"What are you working on now?"

"I don't paint anymore."

Mitch's eyebrows arched in surprise. "Why not?"

"Artsy stuff is for geeks and wimps."

Mitch studied the boy for a moment, then carefully replaced the paintings as a plan slowly took shape in his mind. "I don't know," he said conversationally. "My cousin Jeff—Uncle Ray's son—was a fabulous artist. One of his sculptures won first prize in a contest sponsored by the art museum here in St. Louis."

"Yeah?" A gleam of interest sparked in the teenager's eyes. "I saw that ship in a bottle he did, the one in Uncle Ray's room."

"I forgot all about that," Mitch admitted. "Anyway, he was no nerd. He was a track star on the high school team, and he was voted most-likely-to-succeed by his classmates."

"Well, maybe *all* artsy people aren't geeks," Bruce conceded. "Just most of them."

Mitch was tempted to pursue the subject, but Bruce's sudden yawn made him realize that the boy was exhausted. Not a good time to try to make a point. Besides, he had another type of persuasion in mind. He lifted Bruce's duffel bag and smiled. "Let's go get some shut-eye."

This time there was no disagreement. And once Bruce was settled, Mitch intended to get a couple of hours rest himself before they headed back to the hospital. But first he had a call to make.

* * *

"Why are we stopping here?" Bruce stared at the YMCA building, then turned to Mitch.

"I thought we could both use a little exercise after being cooped up in the hospital all afternoon."

Tess had looked remarkably improved when they'd returned to the hospital around lunchtime with an oversize bouquet. But by four o'clock she was tiring, and Bruce was becoming restless after hours of in-activity. When Mitch suggested that they go get a bite to eat and then return for a brief visit later in the evening, neither Lockwood objected. And it played right into his plan.

"But I didn't bring any gym clothes," Bruce protested.

Mitch glanced at the boy as he set the brake. "That sweat suit is fine for the weight room. Ever done weights before?"

"No."

"I'll show you the ropes." He retrieved his gym bag from the trunk and headed for the front door, leaving Bruce no option but to follow. "Give me a couple of minutes to change," he said over his shoulder as he disappeared into the locker room.

When he returned, in sweatpants and a muscle shirt that revealed well-developed biceps, Bruce looked at him with new respect.

"Do you work out all the time?"

"Not every day. But I try to stay on a schedule. And farm chores definitely build muscles," he added with a grin. "Ready for the tour?"

Mitch led the way to the weight room, where a

couple of other men were already engrossed in their routines. One of them smiled and nodded.

"Hi, Mitch." The man carefully set down the barbells and stood. He was dressed in a sleeveless T-shirt that revealed bulging biceps, and the corded muscles in his legs were clearly visible below his gym shorts.

Mitch returned his greeting. "Joe, I'd like you to meet Bruce Lockwood. He's a student at Southfield High. Bruce, this is Joe Davis."

The man held out his hand, taking Bruce's in a powerful grip. "Nice to meet you, Bruce." Then he directed his gaze at Mitch. "A new recruit for the weight room?"

Mitch grinned. "Yet to be determined. This is his first visit." Mitch folded his arms across his chest consideringly. "You know, I should let *you* show him the ropes. You're the expert."

The man brushed the comment aside. "You know as much about weight lifting as I do."

"Don't listen to him," Mitch told Bruce. "I'm not even in his league. He's won national weight-lifting titles."

Bruce looked in awe at the man across from him. "No kidding?"

"A few," he admitted.

"So how about it? Can you spare a few minutes for an introductory lesson?" Mitch asked.

"Sure. Glad to."

"Thanks. I'll leave you to it, then."

Twenty minutes later, when Mitch was ready to leave, it was clear that Joe had made a friend. He and Bruce were talking animatedly, and Bruce was listening attentively to the man's instructions as he tried out a few simple weight routines.

"I hate to break up the party, but I'm starving," Mitch interrupted, wiping his face on a towel as he joined them.

Joe smiled. "We were done, anyway." He laid his hand on Bruce's shoulder. "We may have a convert here."

Mitch grinned. "I knew you'd do a good sell job. How about joining us for dinner? We're just going to grab something quick."

The man glanced at his watch, then shook his head regretfully. "I'd like to, but I need to finish up here and then head back to the theater. We've got an opening in a week, so we're putting in some extra hours."

"Another time, then. And thanks."

"Yeah. Thanks," Bruce seconded.

"You bet."

Bruce was waiting when Mitch returned from the locker room after a quick shower, and he fell into step beside the older man as they left the Y.

"Is Joe an actor?"

Mitch chuckled. "Hardly. He did try it briefly, though. But as he once told me, it was a good thing the days of throwing rotten tomatoes were long gone by the time he set foot on stage."

"So what did he mean about the theater, then?"

"He's a set designer."

Bruce frowned. "You mean like scenery and stuff?"

"That's right." Mitch tossed his gym bag into the back seat and slid behind the wheel. "How does pizza sound?"

"Fine," Bruce replied distractedly, the frown still

furrowing his brow. Several silent moments passed before he spoke again. "So what exactly does Joe do?"

"He paints some of the backdrops himself and oversees the other set painters," Mitch replied. "And he knows a lot about construction, because he designs the platforms and framework for the sets and supervises the carpenters who build them. He's a pretty versatile guy."

Silence again while Bruce pondered that new information. Not until they pulled into the restaurant parking lot did Mitch finally get the question he'd been hoping for. "Do you think maybe someday...if he had time, I mean...he might show me some of the stuff he works on at the theater?"

"I think he'd be happy to," Mitch replied. "How about if I give him a call and ask?"

"Yeah. That would be cool." For a moment the boy fiddled with the seat belt, and then he took a deep breath as he reached to open his door. "Thanks."

The word was said begrudgingly and without eye contact. But that single syllable meant a lot to Mitch. Because it marked a first in their relationship. And maybe a turning point, as well.

"Are you sure you'll be okay, Mom?"

Tess looked at her son with affection. In the two weeks since her surgery he'd been like a mother hen, waiting on her hand and foot. He'd done the laundry, gone to the grocery store, even laid out her breakfast before he left for school each day. She had been touched—and proud. Bruce was once again the boy she'd always known—helpful, kind, considerate, loving. It gave her new hope that he was beginning to turn a corner, that the clouds over these past difficult months were starting to lift.

She was glad she had *that* hope to cling to. Because the *other* hope, the one that had nothing to do with being a mom and everything to do with being a woman, was slowly slipping away. For a brief moment in time, foolish though it had been, she'd allowed herself to believe that maybe the years ahead might not be so lonely. That maybe she'd met a man who could someday come to love her and want to share her life. Of course, Bruce's relationship with Mitch had been a major hurdle. But in the past couple of weeks the tension between the two of them had eased. Unfortunately, *her* relationship with the handsome principal had taken the opposite turn.

"Mom?"

Tess realized she hadn't answered Bruce's question, heard the undertone of anxiety in his voice and smiled. She didn't want his time at the farm overshadowed by unnecessary worry.

"I'll be fine," she assured him firmly. "I feel almost back to normal."

The doorbell rang, and Tess started to rise from the couch.

"I'll get it, Mom," Bruce told her.

She didn't protest. His willingness to answer the door, as well as his eagerness to visit the farm, were a far cry from his hostile attitude before their first visit. In fact, in the past two weeks his whole attitude had undergone an amazing turnaround. And she had Mitch to thank for it. Not only had he brought Uncle Ray into their lives and watched over her son when she was in the hospital, he'd also found a way to reawaken Bruce's interest in art—something Tess had tried without success to do. Mitch and Bruce had made more than one visit to the local repertory theater to get a behind-the-scenes-look at scenic design, and much to Tess's surprise, Bruce had agreed to help paint sets for the spring play at school. That, in turn, had exposed him to an entirely different social group—and left him little time to hang around with his old gang. No question about it—Tess owed Mitch big time. Her early intuition that he could help Bruce straighten out his life had been right on target.

Unfortunately, her intuition about Mitch's interest in *her* had been way off base. It wasn't that he was uncaring. He'd called frequently to see how she was and stopped by several times with take-out dinners for them. But something…some subtle nuance in their relationship…had changed over the past two weeks. The day he'd stood by her hospital bed after the surgery she'd been sure that his interest went beyond friendship. But she'd finally been forced to acknowledge that the attraction she had thought she'd glimpsed in his eyes must simply have been a side effect of the anesthesia. And that she'd also misread his earlier warmth and friendliness for something more.

The important thing, however, was the change in Bruce, she reminded herself firmly. After all, she could deal with her own hurt. She hadn't been able to deal with Bruce. Thank heaven Mitch had. He'd gone way above and beyond the call of duty by getting personally involved in Bruce's problems. And if that personal involvement didn't extend to Bruce's mom—well, what had she expected, really? She was just an average-looking divorced mother struggling to make ends meet. Not exactly the type of person likely to attract a dynamic, accomplished man like Mitch.

And yet, as he stepped into the room she couldn't stop herself from searching his eyes, hoping yet again to see something that simply wasn't there. The familiar spasm of disappointment in her heart was as real as the pain she'd felt the night of her appendicitis attack.

"How's the patient today?"

With an effort, she summoned up a too-bright smile. "No longer a patient. In fact, I'll be back at work next week while you two gentlemen are enjoying country life."

Mitch frowned. "That seems a bit fast."

"I don't plan to overdo it," she assured him. "But I can sit at a keyboard and write copy just fine."

"I wish you could come with us, mom," Bruce added.

"So do I, hon. But duty calls. I've had two whole weeks to lie around and take it easy. And I'll be down next weekend, like I promised."

Actually, she wished she could back out of that commitment. But when Uncle Ray had called to formally invite Bruce, and then presented a convincing argument that a couple of days in the country would be just the thing to speed up her recuperation, she'd given in. Of course, that had been over a week ago, before she'd finally admitted to herself that Mitch's interest in her was strictly friendship. If her own feelings were stronger...well, that was her problem. And it wasn't fair to disappoint her son just because she was having a hard time coping with her feelings.

Those feelings had also made it difficult to think of a way to thank Mitch for his help during her recuperation. Few principals would take a student into their own home when a parent became ill, even for one night. Not to mention all of the take-out dinners he'd dropped off for them during the past couple of weeks. She owed him more than a simple thank-you note.

At first she'd planned to invite him over for a home-cooked meal. But now that seemed too personal somehow. She'd finally settled on inviting him to dinner at one of the nicer local restaurants. And she would make it very clear that it was just a friendly thank-you. Because the last thing she wanted to do was put him in the awkward position of having to deal with a woman whose feelings he didn't share.

When Bruce hefted his backpack into position, clearly eager to be on the road, Mitch grinned. "Looks like you're ready."

The ghost of an answering smile hovered around Bruce's lips. "Yeah."

"You may not be so eager once Uncle Ray puts you to work," Mitch teased. "He can be a hard taskmaster. I have a feeling he has a list of chores for us a mile long."

"That's okay. I don't mind."

"Is this the same person who complains about taking out the trash?" Tess kidded her son.

"That's different, Mom. This will be fun." He turned to Mitch. "Do you want me to load my stuff in the car?"

"Sure. I need to talk to your mother for a minute, anyway."

He'd given her the perfect opportunity to issue the dinner invitation, Tess realized as Bruce headed out the front door. She took a deep breath and tried to quiet the thumping of her heart as Mitch walked closer. He stopped a couple of feet away, frowned and shoved his hands into his pockets.

"Are you really sure you'll be okay alone for a few days?"

She nodded. "Absolutely." Her voice sounded a bit breathless, and she struggled for a more normal tone. "Besides, you guys will only be an hour away if I really need anything."

"You'll call if you do?"

"Of course."

He paused, as if trying to decide whether he believed her or not, then let it drop. "Okay. We'll check in every day. And I'll be back Thursday. I need to put in a couple days of work, even if it is spring break. I plan to head back down early on Saturday, so I'll pick you up about eight, if that's okay."

"Fine." It was now or never, she realized, forcing herself to take a deep, steadying breath. "Mitch, I— I can't thank you enough for all you've done for Bruce and me over the past couple of weeks. I know how busy you are, and I'm sorry we added to the demands on your time. But I honestly don't know how we'd have managed without you."

An odd light flickered in his eyes, so briefly that Tess wondered if she'd imagined it. "I was glad to help."

She was struck by the husky quality in his voice, but too distracted by what she was about to say to analyze it. "The thing is, I know I can never repay you for your kindness. But I'd like to at least say 'thank you' in some sort of concrete way. So I thought...that is, if you can spare a couple of hours...I'd like to treat you to dinner Friday night.''

For a moment Mitch seemed taken aback by the invitation. ''You don't have to do that, Tess.''

''I know I don't. But I'd like to. You've been a good friend to us, Mitch, and I want you to know that we value that friendship.''

Their gazes locked, but his eyes were shuttered, giving Tess no clue what was going through his mind. She tried desperately to follow his lead and keep her eyes from reflecting the feelings in her heart. But she had no idea if she succeeded.

He looked at her for a long moment, clearly engaged in a silent debate, while she held her breath. Part of her hoped he would accept. Part of her hoped he would decline. Logically speaking, the latter was certainly preferable. Why prolong one-on-one contact when the attraction was one-sided? That was only an exercise in frustration. But good manners had compelled her to issue the invitation, so she'd done her duty. Now the ball was in his court.

''Is it okay if I take some painting stuff to the farm? Just in case I have time?''

There was a momentary pause before Mitch broke eye contact with her to look at Bruce, who was already clutching his easel in his hands. ''Sure. I don't think Uncle Ray expects you to work every minute.''

''Great! Thanks!''

''I'll be right with you.''

''Bye, Mom.''

Before she could respond, Bruce disappeared out

the door. She turned back to Mitch and forced her stiff lips into a smile. "I hope Uncle Ray doesn't regret this. Bruce could tire him out by the end of the week. He's got an unbelievably high energy level when he's interested in something."

"I'm not worried. Those two seem to understand each other. I think they'll set their own limits."

"Well, just give me a call if I need to talk to Bruce."

"I will." He paused, and the expression in his eyes shifted again. *Troubled* was the word that came to Tess's mind. "I appreciate the offer of dinner, Tess," he said slowly. "It's just that I don't want you to feel under any obligation. It was an emergency, and I was glad to help. You'd have done the same thing if the situation was reversed."

"That doesn't mean I appreciate it any less," she countered, then tried for a joking tone. "Besides, Caroline told me about a great restaurant, and this would give me an excuse to try it."

When she mentioned the name, his eyebrows rose. "It is a great restaurant. Also very pricey."

Did he think she couldn't afford dinner for two at a nice restaurant, she wondered? She sat up a little straighter, and her chin tilted up ever so slightly as her pride kicked in. "I can afford an occasional splurge, Mitch. Especially for a special occasion. Like thanking a friend for a very generous favor."

A muscle in his jaw twitched. "I didn't mean to imply you couldn't afford it, Tess." He paused and took a deep breath. "How about this? I'll check with you Thursday, and if you're feeling up to it, it's a date."

Hardly, she thought. But at least she had her answer. "That's fine." She hadn't meant to sound put out, but she couldn't prevent a slight touch of coolness from creeping into her voice.

Mitch raked his fingers through his hair, his expression contrite. "Look, Tess, I didn't mean to sound ungracious. I really do appreciate the invitation."

"It's okay."

"No, it's not. And I'm sorry."

It suddenly occurred to Tess that not once during her ten-year marriage to Peter had her husband ever apologized for anything. He seemed to feel that acknowledging a mistake somehow diminished him. But Tess viewed it in exactly the opposite way. To her, the ability to admit mistakes, to say "I'm sorry," increased a person's stature. Her expression softened and she smiled. "Accepted."

"I'll call you, then?"

"That would be fine. And Mitch…keep an eye on Bruce, okay?"

"Count on it. He'll be in good hands."

Of that she had no doubt.

"I'd say that was one tuckered-out youngster. I'd be willing to bet he was out cold the minute his head hit the pillow."

Mitch chuckled as he joined Uncle Ray on the porch swing, savoring a long, slow sip of coffee as they enjoyed the unseasonably warm spring evening. "I warned him you were a slave driver."

Uncle Ray smiled. "You should have seen me in my heyday."

Mitch gave an exaggerated groan. "I don't think my back would have survived."

Now it was Uncle Ray's turn to chuckle. "Hard work is good for the soul. And the body."

"You may have a hard time convincing Bruce of that tomorrow when he can barely move."

"That boy is a hard worker, I'll say that for him. Willing to tackle anything. And he put in a full day. Nice young man, too. Not too many boys his age would give up a Saturday, let alone a whole spring break, to work on a farm with an old man."

"He likes you."

Uncle Ray looked pleased. "I like him, too."

"I wish he felt the same about me."

"Maybe he does."

Mitch shook his head. "No way. I'm the authority figure who's been cramping his style."

"You're also the friend who helped him out when his mom was sick and who introduced him to Joe Davis. He mentions him every time he e-mails me. That was a brilliant move on your part."

Mitch shrugged. "I was lucky I knew someone who could tap into Bruce's talent. And I was lucky Joe was willing to cooperate."

"I take it that the episode at the Y wasn't a chance meeting."

Mitch hesitated, then shook his head. "No."

"Didn't think so. I could see your hand in it. It was a nice thing to do, son."

"I was just glad I finally hit on something that seemed to reach him. He was definitely heading for trouble, and Tess was at her wit's end."

"Mmm. Hard thing, raising a boy that age alone. I don't envy her."

"Single parenthood is never easy," Mitch concurred. "But from what she's told me, they're better off without Bruce's father. I have a feeling he did more harm than good—to both of them."

Uncle Ray shook his head. "Makes you wonder, doesn't it? Bruce is a great kid. And even though I don't know Tess all that well, she sure seems like a nice person. Conscientious and genuine and caring."

"She is."

"Can't imagine why any man would let someone like her slip away."

"Me, neither."

Silence fell as the two men swung gently, a comfortable stillness born of secrets shared, absolute trust and mutual respect. Several minutes passed before Uncle Ray spoke.

"I've got some news for you, son."

Something in the older man's voice put Mitch on alert, momentarily driving thoughts of Tess out of his mind. "What is it?"

"I've sold the farm."

With an instinct honed long ago Mitch had braced himself for bad news. But his uncle's calm announcement stunned him. "What?"

"I've sold the farm," Uncle Ray repeated. "At least, most of it. I kept the five acres around the house and barn."

"But why?" Mitch couldn't even conceive of his uncle without the farm, or vice versa.

"Because it was time, son." The older man's voice was quiet but firm.

"But…but this is your life."

"It *was* my life," Uncle Ray corrected him. "And it was a good one. But also a hard one. I'm getting older, Mitch. I can't keep up with things anymore."

"But I'm more than happy to help."

"I know that. But I can't expect you to spend what little free time you have out here. You need to live your own life, not help me keep memories of my old one alive. The Lord and I had a long talk about this, and I know it's the right thing to do."

Mitch felt as if someone had kicked him in the gut. "You mean you did this for me?"

"Partly. But only partly," he clarified. "Mostly I did it for me. And that's the truth, Mitch. The fact is, time brings changes. People change. Circumstances change. And sometimes you just have to realize that it's time to move on."

*Time to move on.* The words echoed in Mitch's heart, and he stared down into his coffee.

"It's not an easy thing, letting go, is it, son?" His uncle's voice was gentle, and Mitch suddenly knew they weren't talking about the farm anymore. He turned, and though the light was dim, the kindness and understanding in the older man's eyes were clear.

"Not everyone has your courage, Uncle Ray," he replied quietly.

"You do."

Mitch shook his head. "I'm not so sure."

"I am. And I'm sure about something else, too. You shouldn't spend the rest of your life alone. And lonely."

For once Mitch didn't deny his loneliness. He'd dealt with it successfully for years, but lately the emptiness of his personal life had become oppressive, leaving him keenly aware of the hollow echo in his heart.

Mitch rose and walked restlessly to the edge of the porch, planting his hands on the railing as he stared out into the darkness. "So what are you saying, Uncle Ray?"

"You know."

Yeah, he knew. Mitch drew a deep breath and let it out slowly. "I said I'd never get involved with anyone again."

"That was years ago, son. And Tess seems like a real special woman. The kind that doesn't come around very often."

He knew that, too. "She asked me to dinner."

There was a moment of silence. "Are you going?"

"I don't know."

"Why not?"

Mitch drew in a deep breath, let it out slowly. As usual, his uncle had honed right to the heart of the matter. "Because I'm afraid."

"Of what?"

"Messing things up. Making the same mistakes. Hurting the people I love. Just like before."

"That was a long time ago, son."

"I'm the same man."

"Are you?"

Mitch thought about that. Was he? Hadn't he learned a great deal—about selflessness and sensitivity and listening—during the intervening years? Hadn't he learned to recognize what was precious and cherish it? Or was he just kidding himself that he'd grown and changed and become a better person?

''I don't know,'' he said at last with a sigh.

''Well, I do. And the answer is no. You're not the same person you were six years ago. No one is. That's why I'm selling the farm. Because it's time to move on. Maybe it's time for you to do the same.''

Mitch didn't respond. But in his heart he acknowledged the truth of Uncle Ray's words. Though he'd always vowed never again to get involved with anyone, Tess had made him rethink that pledge. Because Uncle Ray was also right about her. She was special. Very special.

Mitch knew all that. Knew that he needed to revisit the decision he'd made six years ago, when his life was an emotional hell. Knew that if he didn't pursue his interest in Tess, he could very well lose the chance to build a new life. Knew, also, that he might very well let this opportunity pass him by, even if it meant spending the rest of his life alone.

Because the bottom line was, he was just plain scared.

# *Chapter Nine*

Tess checked her watch and frowned. Mitch was fifteen minutes late. It seemed highly unlikely that he'd forgotten their dinner date, considering that he'd called to confirm the time yesterday. He'd even offered to pick her up, but she'd figured it was safer simply to meet him at the restaurant. Since he wasn't the type to stand someone up, something must have detained him at the office.

Tess looked around the lounge of the upscale restaurant, where the maître d' had suggested she wait, and shifted uncomfortably in her seat. She felt out of her element amid the cozy twosomes and intimate laughter coming from the small, candlelit tables. A more casual place would have been far more appropriate for a thank-you dinner than this romantic dining establishment, with its dim light, elegant rose-colored decor and mellow background music, she realized. Had Caroline purposely set her up? Her boss had hinted more than once that Tess should consider the handsome principal in more than a professional light, but Tess had always sidestepped the suggestion. Maybe this was Caroline's not-so-subtle way of giving her a little push in what she considered the right direction, Tess mused wryly.

She just hoped Mitch didn't interpret it that way. His voice had still sounded a bit cautious on the phone when he'd called to confirm their dinner, and she'd been tempted once again to offer him an out. But something had held her back. So here she was, meeting a friend to repay a debt in what was clearly a place designed to foster romance.

Tess glanced yet again at her watch. Mitch was now twenty minutes late. They'd agreed on an early dinner, since she still tired easily, and he'd said he would come straight from his office. It was time to call, she decided.

Tess reached for her purse and stood. But she'd walked no more than two steps toward the foyer when she suddenly froze. Though she hadn't seen him in years, and his once-ebony hair now contained glints of silver, there was no question about the identity of the man who stood on the threshold of the lounge, coolly surveying the occupants.

It was Peter, her ex-husband.


"I'm glad you stopped by, Tony." Mitch laid his hand on the boy's shoulder as they walked toward the office reception area.

"Yeah. Me, too."

"My door's always open, you know."

"Yeah. But it's easier to stop by when school's out."

"The guys give you a hard time about talking to me, I take it."

The fourteen-year-old shrugged. "You know how it is."

"Unfortunately, I do." He paused on the threshold and looked at Tony. "Hang in there, okay? I know things aren't great at home, but there are a lot of people who care about you. Including me. Don't forget that. And I'm here if you need me, anytime, day or night. You've got my home number, right?"

"Yeah."

"Will you stop in and see me again next week?"

"I'll try."

"We can meet somewhere away from here if that's easier, okay?"

"Yeah. Thanks, Mr. Jackson."

"You bet. Just remember that I'm here for you."

"I will. See ya."

Mitch watched the teenager cross the small reception room, then glanced toward Karen's desk, a troubled expression on his face. "I worry about him."

"You worry about all of them," she countered as she pushed her keyboard under the desk.

"Some more than others."

"Are things still bad at home?"

"Yeah."

She raised one eyebrow knowingly. "I'm not surprised. I heard his mother just got a big promotion. She'll probably be around even less now. Which means his dad will drink more than ever."

Mitch looked at her and shook his head incredulously. "How do you know so much about everything?"

"Certainly no thanks to you," she retorted. "You never tell me anything."

"If I want the kids to trust me, I have to keep their confidences."

She grinned. "I know. I'm just giving you a hard time. I know something else, too."

"What?"

"You're late for your six-o'clock appointment."

Mitch glanced at his watch, muttered something under his breath, then turned and strode toward his desk. He stuffed a handful of papers into his briefcase, sparing only a brief glance for Karen, who had followed in a more leisurely fashion. She surveyed him from the doorway, one shoulder propped against the door frame, arms folded over her chest.

Mitch looked at her again as he snapped his briefcase shut, noting her amused expression. "What?" he asked.

"Considering it's Friday night, and considering that classy suit and tie you're wearing, I have a feeling that *appointment* may be too businesslike a term for whatever you have planned for tonight."

He flashed her a grin as he shrugged into a gray pinstripe jacket. "Fishing?"

"Maybe."

"They're not biting tonight."

"Maybe not here. But this isn't the only fishing hole in town."

Mitch chuckled. "I told you before, Karen. You missed your calling. Are you sure you don't want me to put you in touch with my FBI contacts? They could use more good agents."

"Ha, ha. Very funny. So are you going to fess up,

or do I have to keep fishing?'' When Mitch silently picked up his briefcase and headed for the door, Karen sighed and stepped aside. ''Okay, have it your way. But the truth will come out.''

As he passed his secretary, Mitch winked. ''Good luck.''

She grinned. ''You, too. And by the way—it's about time.''

*Please, God, don't let him see me!* Tess prayed silently but fervently. Peter was the last person she wanted to see, especially tonight. Not when she was already nervous about her dinner plans with Mitch. Not when she was so unprepared for a verbal sparring match with her ex-husband. Not when she needed every ounce of the confidence she had so painstakingly rebuilt after Peter's masterful job of destroying it. Just being in his presence made her feel insecure and shaky.

She glanced around desperately, hoping there was an alcove, a ladies' room, anything that would offer her an escape so she could mentally regroup.

''Tess?''

Too late. With dread she turned slowly to face the man who had once been her husband. He strolled over, and his gaze blatantly raked over her—cold, assessing, critical. He hadn't changed a bit, she thought bitterly. ''It *is* you. I wasn't sure. You look more gaunt than I remember.''

Not ''How are you?'' or ''Nice to see you.'' Just a derogatory comment. She should have been used to it by now. Should have developed a skin tough enough to deflect his barbs. Yet they still had the power to sting. And intimidate.

"Hello, Peter." She tried for a cool, aloof tone, but couldn't quite pull it off. "What are you doing here?"

He knew exactly what she meant, but chose to play games, as he always had. "Meeting a couple of colleagues for a drink."

"I mean in St. Louis."

"Why didn't you say so? I'm in town for a convention. Just for a couple of days. I'm leaving tomorrow."

It suddenly occurred to Tess that Peter hadn't even let his son know he would be in town. Had made no attempt to see or even call him while he was here. A deep, seething anger swept over her, and this time the coolness in her tone was real.

"I'm surprised you didn't call."

He gave her a smirk. "Don't tell me you've been missing me."

"Don't flatter yourself. I wasn't thinking of me."

For a moment his face went blank, and then, for one brief moment, he had the decency to look embarrassed. "Oh, yeah. How is the kid?"

Her knuckles whitened on her purse. "His name is Bruce," she said tersely. "Or have you forgotten that, too?"

"Same smart mouth, I see," he sneered. "You always were a master at dishing out guilt." He glanced pointedly at the bare fingers of her left hand. "I'm not surprised you never remarried. No man wants to have someone constantly lecturing to him. Believe me, there are plenty of women out there a lot better looking than you who know how to make a man feel good about himself.''

Tess's temples began to throb, and her legs suddenly felt shaky. The memories of her unhappy, bitter years with this man who was now little more than a stranger came rushing back, leaving a sick feeling in the pit of her stomach. Dear God, how had she managed to put up with his vitriolic verbal abuse for ten long years?

Tess had never been very good at hiding her feelings, and she knew from the smirk on Peter's face that he'd correctly deduced that his barbs had hit home. ''So what are you doing in a classy place like this, anyway? Reporters must be getting paid more than they used to.''

''Tess! Sorry I'm late. I got held up at the office.''

Tess felt the comfort of a protective arm around her shoulders, and she turned, her throat tightening with emotion. He might not be wearing a suit of shining armor, but as far as she was concerned Mitch was every bit the knight rescuing the damsel in distress.

Mitch looked down into her eyes, and his gut clenched. He had hesitated on the sidelines when he'd discovered Tess talking with Peter, thinking that perhaps she'd run into an old friend. But her tense body posture quickly put that theory to rest. The man was no friend. Mitch had moved closer, and though he'd picked up only part of the conversation, it had been enough for him to identify the man—and for a white-hot anger to erupt inside him. Tess had implied that her ex-husband was insensitive and uncaring. But what Mitch had witnessed went beyond that. The man was arrogant. Conceited. Self-centered. And abusive.

He had hurt Tess before. Deeply. Now he was doing it again. And Mitch had no intention of letting him get away with it. Without even stopping to consider his actions, he leaned down and brushed his lips across hers. He didn't wait to assess her reaction, but instead smoothly transferred his gaze to Peter.

As Mitch had anticipated, the gesture wasn't lost on Tess's ex-husband. The other man's eyes narrowed appraisingly, and there was a glimmer of admiration in them when he spoke again to Tess. As if Mitch's interest in Tess somehow made her more worthy of his respect, Mitch thought with disgust.

"Are you going to introduce your…friend?" Peter prompted.

Tess was still trying to recover from Mitch's unexpected kiss and the brief but breathtaking sensation of his lips on hers that had, for just a second, made her completely forget that Peter was standing only inches away. She turned back to her ex-husband, taking comfort in the shelter of Mitch's arm, and quickly made the introductions.

When Peter extended his hand, Mitch hesitated. Finally, with obvious reluctance, he withdrew his arm from around her shoulders. As soon as the brief handshake was completed, however, he reached over and entwined his fingers with hers, noting the coldness of her hand and the tremors that ran through it.

"Nice to meet you, Mitch. Can I buy you both a drink?"

Tess looked at Peter in disgust. He hadn't changed one bit. Jovial and considerate in public, an ogre in private. Would Mitch be fooled, as so many others had been? she wondered.

"Sorry, we're already late for our dinner reservations."

"Another time, maybe."

Mitch ignored that comment and turned to Tess. The smile he gave her was warm and intimate. "You look fabulous tonight. New dress?"

She looked at him in surprise. Actually, it was. She hadn't intended to buy anything new for tonight. But she'd seen a dress in the window of a small shop and hadn't been able to resist. The simple, elegant lines of the black cocktail dress were suited to her slender curves, and the moment she'd slipped it over her head she'd felt young and attractive and more woman than mom. It had been a foolish extravagance, of course, but it had done wonders for her self-esteem. Until Peter's opening comment about her gauntness, which had quickly deflated her ego. But Mitch's appreciative gaze helped restore her shaky self-confidence, even if it was only a gallant act for Peter's benefit.

"Yes."

He gave her a lazy smile, then reached up and gently brushed a wayward strand of hair back from her face. "I like it."

"So, you two seem like old friends."

Mitch frowned, as if he'd completely forgotten the other man was there and was annoyed at being interrupted. He spared him only a quick glance, and once again ignored his remark as he turned back to Tess. "Ready for dinner?"

"Yes."

"I think our table is ready."

His hand still linked with hers, he deliberately turned away from Peter and led the way toward the dining room. Tess followed his lead, turning for a brief parting look at Peter. Her ex's face was slightly ruddy, and his eyes glinted with anger. The picture of a man clearly not accustomed to having his charm rebuffed. As Tess turned away, she couldn't help but feel vindicated. Mitch hadn't been fooled. He had seen right through Peter and had very clearly put him in his place.

As they took their seats at the linen-covered table, the waiter smiled in greeting. "Can I get either of you something from the bar while you look over the menu?"

Mitch glanced at Tess questioningly.

"Just water, please," she said.

"How about some wine?" Mitch suggested.

Tess didn't drink much. But if ever there was a night for it, this was it. "That would be nice."

"I'll bring a wine menu, sir," the waiter offered.

When he left, Tess drew a shaky breath and gave Mitch an apologetic look. "Sorry about that. I had no idea he was even in town."

"So I gathered. And I'm the one who's sorry. I heard enough to get a very clear picture of your ex's character. I'm sorry he upset you."

Tess tried for a smile, but barely pulled it off. "It was that obvious, huh?"

"To me."

"And to him. Which was exactly what he intended." She combed her fingers through her hair distractedly, then clasped her hands tightly together on the table in front of her. "More than anything, though, I'm angry at myself that I still let him do that to me, after all these years."

"Some scars run deep."

"Yes, they do. Thank you for stepping in, Mitch. I was sinking fast."

"You would have been fine."

"I don't know," she said doubtfully. "I can't believe he can still make me feel so…unworthy, somehow. Of respect. Of consideration. Of love. It wasn't until you came along that he looked at me with anything but contempt."

"You didn't need me to validate your worth."

"I agree with you, in theory. And in my heart. But you're right—some scars do run deep." She closed her eyes and gave a little shudder. "I had forgotten just how bad he could make me feel with only a word or a look." She took a deep breath, and when she opened her eyes, she could see the concern in his. Again she tried for a smile. "I really am sorry, Mitch. I wanted to give you a pleasant evening, not force you to deal with ghosts from my past."

Instinctively he reached over and laid his hand over hers. His eyes grew warm and his smile was genuine. "The evening is young, Tess. And ghosts don't scare me." For a moment his own eyes clouded, but they cleared so quickly she wondered if it had just been a play of light from the flickering candle on their table. "Now, how about that wine?" he suggested as he gave her clasped hands a gentle squeeze, then released them to open the menu.

After that, the evening seemed to fly. The food was good. The pianist excellent. The atmosphere relaxing. Her tension gradually melted away, leaving her feeling peaceful and happy. Or had her mellow state of mind been induced by the wine? Tess wasn't sure.

All she knew was that she was having one of the most pleasant evenings of her life. Mitch was warm and witty, and their conversation ranged from politics to music to favorite vacations. They talked about Uncle Ray and Bruce. About their own childhoods. About philosophy and history and art. About the importance of faith in their lives. And they discovered they had amazingly similar tastes and values. It was one of those evenings she wished would never end.

Mitch seemed to feel the same way. Only after they'd lingered over their coffee and dessert did he finally, reluctantly, look at his watch.

Tess savored the last bite of her dessert, feeling completely at ease and relaxed. "What time is it?"

"Ten o'clock."

Her eyes widened. "You're kidding!"

"I wish I was."

Carefully she laid her fork down, trying to hide her disappointment. "Well, we do have an early day tomorrow. I guess we should go."

"I guess so."

But neither made a move to rise. Tess risked a look at Mitch, and their gazes locked. Oddly enough, she saw conflict in his eyes. As if he was wrestling with a difficult problem. What was he thinking? she wondered. And what did he see in her eyes? Liking? Yearning? Attraction? Heaven help her, she hoped not! But since all of those things were in her heart, they might well be reflected in her eyes.

As Mitch gazed at the woman across from him, he struggled to reconcile his conflicting desires. Earlier she'd seemed vulnerable, and he'd wanted to protect her. During dinner her unaffected charm and spontaneity made him want to learn everything about her. Now, as the evening waned and her eyes grew luminous in the candlelight, he just plain wanted. He wanted to feel her soft hair against his cheek. He wanted to run his hands over her silky skin. He wanted to hold her so close that they would forget the past, the present and the future. He wanted no barriers between them.

And there lay the problem. Physical barriers could be dispensed with. But the secrets and the ghosts would remain, making true intimacy impossible. Mitch sighed. It was definitely time to say good-night.

But Tess spoke first, in a voice that was hesitant and uncertain. "I know we drove separately, but I—I have some Irish Cream liqueur at home if you'd like to stop by for a nightcap before calling it a night."

Mitch took a deep breath. Dear Lord, how much willpower was a man supposed to have? he pleaded silently. How could he refuse the very invitation his heart yearned for? But he had to be firm, he told himself resolutely. He had to stay the course he'd set six years before. *He had to!*

Yet when he spoke, his heart betrayed him. "That sounds great."

The words stunned both of them. Tess clearly hadn't been expecting him to accept her invitation, and Mitch couldn't believe he had.

"I'll just follow you home in my car," he added.

And so he did, Tess noted, her gaze moving back and forth between the rearview mirror and the road in front of her. And with every block she drove, her panic grew. What was she getting herself into? She had asked Mitch to her apartment for one simple reason—a desire to extend one of the most perfect evenings of her life. Her motives were straightforward. The real question was, why had he accepted? And what did he expect? She wished she knew!

So did Mitch. As he drove through the darkness behind her, he asked himself those same questions. He liked Tess. A lot. He enjoyed her company. He admired her spunk and courage. She made him feel happy and somehow whole.

But the real reason he'd accepted her invitation was because he was powerfully attracted to her. To pretend otherwise would be foolish. She made him feel things he hadn't felt in a very long time, fueled the flames of longing he'd so carefully banked. But Tess didn't fit into his plans. So it would be better to keep his distance before the flames she was fanning to life erupted into a white-hot blaze. And yet here he was putting himself in a position that could very easily get out of hand.

Mitch sighed. For six years he'd put his life in the Lord's hands and resolved to devote himself to helping teens find the right path—to the exclusion of pretty much everything and everyone else, other than Uncle Ray. And he'd stuck to it resolutely. Yet tonight he'd accepted Tess's invitation for a nightcap. Which was clearly a mistake. One of the lessons he'd learned as a cop was that the best way to avoid danger was to stay away from dangerous situations if at all possible and to proceed with extreme caution when danger couldn't be avoided. It was a cardinal rule.

And it was a rule he'd just broken.

# *Chapter Ten*

By the time Tess set the parking brake and took a couple of deep breaths, Mitch had pulled in beside her. A moment later he opened her door.

"I won't stay long," he said, his voice huskier than it had been at the restaurant. "You need your rest."

She looked up at him, but in the dim light it was impossible to discern the expression in his eyes. Nevertheless, she felt reassured that he hadn't interpreted her invitation for a drink as an invitation for something more.

He accompanied her to the door, his hand resting lightly and protectively in the small of her back, and Tess thought again about how he had come to her rescue earlier in the evening. And how right and good this man's touch felt.

Until she'd met Mitch, she'd successfully stifled her needs, had put all her energies into raising her son and creating a stable home life for them. Then had come her problems with Bruce. Problems that stemmed not from lack of trying or insufficient commitment on her part, but from long-ago hurts inflicted on her son by the man Mitch had so accurately assessed and dispensed with tonight. Without the man beside her, Tess wasn't sure where Bruce would be right now. Mitch had brought Uncle Ray into their lives and found the key to unlock Bruce's artistic talents—two great blessings for which she would be forever grateful.

Tess knew how she felt about what Mitch had done for Bruce. She wasn't as sure how to feel about what he'd done for her. To her. Because of Mitch, she'd lain awake for too many nights, tense, lonely, wanting. Because of Mitch, she'd begun to realize just what a difference the right man might have made in her life. Because of Mitch, she'd begun to believe once again in the possibility of fairy-tale endings. Because of Mitch, she felt more like a woman than a mother for the first time in years.

None of those were bad things, she supposed. But Mitch and Bruce still had issues to work out between them, and she wasn't at all sure about Mitch's feelings for her. Early on, she'd thought she'd detected interest in his eyes. Attraction, possibly. But since her surgery, he'd grown more distant, despite his act tonight in front of Peter. He'd obviously heard enough of the conversation to realize how little Peter thought of her, had most likely heard the man's remark about her still-single state—and the reason for it. Mitch had meant to neutralize the biting words of her ex-husband, to throw them back in his face and show him how wrong he was, and he'd succeeded. It was a noble gesture, handled with taste and tenderness, and it had touched her deeply. She just wished it had been motivated by more than nobility.

They paused at the threshold of the apartment while Tess fitted her key in the lock, then Mitch followed her inside.

''Make yourself comfortable,'' she said over her shoulder. ''I'll get the drinks.''

By the time she reappeared with two glasses, Mitch had removed his jacket and was checking out her meager supply of CDs. He extracted one and held it up as he turned to her.

''You didn't tell me you were a fan of Satchmo.''

She smiled. ''Didn't I? I'm surprised. We talked about everything else tonight.''

''Do you mind if I put this on?''

''Not at all. I like a little Louis Armstrong late at night.''

A moment later the gravelly voice of the singer, backed by mellow jazz, filled the room, and Mitch joined her on the couch.

''I ditched the jacket. I hope you don't mind.''

''You can do the same with the tie if you'd be more comfortable.''

He grinned. ''A woman after my own heart.'' He reached up and loosened the tie, but left it in place. ''*Much* better.''

She swirled her drink, glanced down and took a deep breath. ''Mitch…thank you again for tonight.''

He tilted his head and looked at her quizzically. ''I think that's my line. *You* treated *me*.''

''I mean about Peter. For pretending that we were…that you were my…'' She flushed and grasped her drink with both hands to steady them. ''You know what I mean. Anyway, it…it made me feel sort of…vindicated, I guess…to have him think that maybe he wasn't the only one who was attractive to the opposite sex.''

Mitch studied her, a slight frown marring his brow. ''There are no maybes about it, Tess. You're a beautiful woman. Frankly, I think your ex-husband was an idiot to let you walk away.''

Tess's flush deepened and she took a sip of her drink. When she spoke, her voice was slightly unsteady. ''I was just a tool to Peter. Someone who could help him make the right connections for his work.'' She paused, then took a deep breath to muster her courage. ''He…he never loved me, Mitch. Not even in the beginning.'' There. She'd finally put into words the painful truth that she'd hidden in her heart for years.

Mitch sensed that Tess had just shared something with him that few, if any, had been privy to. Without even stopping to think, he reached over and took her hand, enfolding it in a warm, protective clasp. ''I'm sorry, Tess.'' The simple statement, spoken from the heart, communicated all that needed to be said.

Tess looked down at their entwined hands, and her throat tightened. Gentle, supportive touches like these had never been part of her marriage. Nor had such simple but heartfelt expressions of caring. She swallowed, struggling to hold in check the tears that suddenly welled in her eyes. Tears for all she had missed, and tears of tenderness for this special man.

''Even after all these years, it hurts to say those words,'' she admitted in a choked voice. ''But I don't really think Peter knows how to love. He's always

been too absorbed in his career, assessing and eval-
uating everything in terms of how it might enhance
his advancement opportunities. Bruce and I were just
props. There was nothing between us in the end. No
love. No warmth. No respect.''

''So why did you stay so long, Tess?''

The question was gentle. Curious, not accusatory,
though surely Mitch must think she was a fool to have
endured such a loveless marriage. But she'd had her
reasons, and she looked at him directly. ''Because I'd
taken a vow before God that said for better or worse,
till death do us part. And because I believe in keeping
my promises, Mitch.'' She drew a shaky breath and
once more looked down at her drink. ''I just never
realized how bad the 'worse' part could get.'' Her
voice caught and she closed her eyes, struggling again
to control the tears that threatened to spill down her
cheeks.

Mitch saw the raw anguish in her face, and his gut
clenched painfully even as his grip on her hand tightened. Tess had never told him any details about her
relationship with her ex-husband, only that it had
been bad. And it was clear that Peter had hurt Tess
and Bruce psychologically. But for the first time he
wondered if there was a component of physical abuse,
as well. The very thought that anyone might lay a
hand on this gentle woman filled him with a cold fury
that he had to struggle mightily to control.

''Tess, I know what you told me at the school carnival, and I got a firsthand look at your ex tonight,''
he said as calmly as possible. ''Tell me to mind my
own business if this question is out of line, but…did
he ever physically hurt you or Bruce?''

Tess opened her eyes and looked over at him. There was a fierceness in his expression, a coldness that was at odds with the warmth of his tender touch. As if the thought of any harm coming to her or Bruce mattered to him personally, far beyond his role as a caring principal. Slowly she shook her head, deeply touched by his concern. "No. He never laid a hand on us. I would have walked out sooner if he had. But the scars are still there, Mitch. You just can't see them."

He was quiet for a moment, as if debating whether to ask his next question, but at last he spoke. "Can I ask what finally made you decide to leave?"

She looked at him, into the eyes of this man whom she trusted implicitly. Their deep brown depths radiated strength and integrity. He was the kind of man you could count on. In the three months she'd known him, never once had he been anything but supportive and understanding in his dealings with her. And from what she heard, he was that way with everyone.

Tess gazed down at her drink. Should she trust this special man with her final humiliation or allow it to remain hidden, just as the intricate design on the bottom of her mother's antique glasses was hidden by the opaque liquid? Caution advised her to play it safe and leave the question unanswered. But her heart told her otherwise. And suddenly she knew that it was time to listen to her heart—and to place her trust in the Lord. She took a deep breath and then forced herself to meet his eyes.

"Are you sure you want to know? It's not pretty."

He stroked the back of her hand with his thumb, never relinquishing his hold. "Life isn't sometimes.

And I've seen my share of the sordid side. More than my share, in fact. I'm willing to listen, if you're willing to share.''

Carefully she set her glass on the coffee table, and with a final squeeze of his hand, she extricated hers and rose to walk over to the window. She pulled the drape aside to stare out into the darkness while Mitch waited quietly on the couch behind her. Though they weren't touching, she could feel his support. It was an almost tangible thing, reaching across the distance that separated them, enveloping her with warmth and caring, giving her the courage she needed to begin.

''Bruce was eight at the time,'' she said, striving with only limited success to control the tremor that ran through her voice. ''We'd gone to my parents' house for the weekend to celebrate Bruce's birthday. As usual, Peter said he was too busy to make it. Even though my parents and I did our best to make it a happy weekend, and even though Bruce pretended he didn't care about Peter's absence, I could tell that he was upset by it. So on Sunday I told Bruce we'd head home early and surprise his dad, and that maybe the three of us could go out for a birthday dinner.''

Tess let the drape fall back into place, but still she didn't turn to face Mitch. ''When we got home, there was a strange car parked in the driveway. It didn't really surprise me. Peter worked at all hours of the day and night, seven days a week, so even though it was a Sunday afternoon, I just figured a colleague had stopped by. And that's exactly what had happened.'' Her mouth twisted wryly at the memory. ''His twenty-year-old summer intern, in fact. Only, they weren't working.''

She paused and drew a deep breath. "Fortunately, Peter heard the car and met us in the upstairs hall. He'd barely had time to throw on a robe, and I could see her through the crack in the bedroom door, which wasn't quite closed. She was…in my bed." Tess closed her eyes and wrapped her arms around her body. When she spoke again, her voice was barely a whisper, and Mitch had to lean closer to hear her. "Peter was furious. At *me!* As if I should apologize for catching him in a compromising position." She gave a brief, bitter laugh. "Believe it or not, I almost felt as if I should. But I didn't. I just hustled Bruce out of there, and except for returning to get our things, I never set foot in that house again."

There was a long moment of silence, and then Tess finally found the courage to face Mitch. His mouth was set in a thin, unsmiling line, and she could see the tension in his jaw. "I don't know how many there were before her, Mitch. Probably quite a few. I was completely oblivious. It just never occurred to me that Peter would be unfaithful. I always knew his work came first, that it was his mistress and his first love. I figured no woman could compete with that. But I was wrong. I just wasn't the right woman."

She turned away again to hide the hurt and embarrassment in her eyes, struggling to maintain an even tone. "Needless to say, I was devastated. And humiliated. How could this kind of behavior have been going on—in my own house and in my own *bed*—without my knowledge? I felt like a fool. And I knew then that I had to get out. For my sake and for Bruce's. Peter was just plain bad news. So we left. And we built a new life. And now you have my life s-story.'' Despite her best efforts, her voice broke on the last word.

Mitch was on his feet and beside her in three long strides. Silently he gathered her into his arms and held her close, one hand tangled in her hair, the other wrapped around her slender waist. She was trembling, and for several long moments he simply held her, pressing her cheek against his solid chest as he silently cursed the man who had hurt her so badly.

Tess struggled to control her tears, but finally lost the battle. A ragged sob escaped her lips, and she felt Mitch tighten his grip. She clung to him, drawing comfort from his strong arms and the steady beating of his heart against her ear. Though she'd spent many a lonely night berating Peter in her heart and silently lashing out at him for the devastation he'd wreaked on his family, she'd never let herself cry. She'd told herself that he wasn't worth tears. But now she let them flow. Not for what had been. But for what might have been, with the right man beside her. Like the one now holding her so tenderly in his arms.

Mitch gazed down at the bowed head resting against his chest, and a surge of emotion swept over him. It was almost like…love, he realized with a frown. But how could that be? He and Tess were little more than acquaintances, really. And yet, he couldn't deny the feeling of connection between them at some deep, intrinsic level. As if they were soul mates. This strong woman, who had faced adversity head-on and moved ahead with courage and determination, had made him reexamine his priorities for the first time in six years. Her tenderness had touched his heart, awakening emotions that he'd long ago suppressed. And her touch left him aching with need, igniting a deep, powerful desire that had kept him awake for far too many nights.

Tess moved in his arms then, nestling even closer to him, and warning bells began to flash in his mind. Mitch knew he was on dangerous ground. Knew the self-control he'd always prided himself on was slipping. Knew he had to get out of there. Fast.

But just as he prepared to release his hold on her, Tess tilted her head back and looked up at him. Her tearstained eyes were so trusting, so soft, so filled with love that Mitch was simply left with no option.

He had to kiss her.

Even as Mitch leaned down to her, his brain kicked into overdrive. He told himself to stop. Told himself that he might regret this later. Told himself it was too soon.

And then his lips touched hers, and his brain stopped working. He couldn't have come up with a rational thought if he'd wanted to. Not with the hammering of her heart thudding against his chest. Not with the silky strands of her hair tangled in his hand. Not with her soft sounds of pleasure filling his ears.

No, there was no way he could think, rationally or otherwise. And so he finally admitted defeat and simply gave himself up to the moment.

Tess wasn't sure exactly how they had gone from confession to clinch. All she knew was that when she looked up at Mitch, the hunger in his gaze had crumbled her defenses. The need reflected in his eyes matched that in her own heart, and she simply couldn't fight the attraction any longer. From the beginning, she'd felt drawn to this man. She'd told herself that a relationship with him simply wasn't possible, given her need to put Bruce's interests first. But lately, Bruce's attitude seemed to be softening and she'd begun to hope that maybe something could develop. Now, it seemed, her hopes were being realized far beyond her wildest dreams.

Tess hadn't been kissed in more years than she could count. Peter had stopped kissing her long before their marriage disintegrated, and she'd dated no one since. She'd almost been afraid that she'd forgotten *how* to kiss. But Mitch quickly put those fears to rest. His lips were hungry yet gentle. Tess had never been kissed with such intensity, such focus, and she surprised even herself by her response. A heart-thudding, breathless excitement swept over her as his strong hands pressed her close. The power of her response made her feel euphoric—and suddenly very scared.

The scared part was what finally made her brain turn back on. And fear was what made her tense— ever so slightly, but enough for Mitch to sense the subtle change.

Slowly, reluctantly, he released her lips. With their gazes only inches apart, he studied her eyes. They were hazy with longing, but he couldn't ignore the glimmer of uncertainty in their depths—much as he wanted to. Tess wasn't the kind of woman to share her heart lightly. She'd opened up to him emotionally tonight in ways that had surprised them both, clearly taking more risk than she'd planned. But he could sense that she was now moving beyond her comfort level.

And much as he hated to admit it, she was right. Neither of them needed to rush into anything. In fact, he'd probably taken advantage of her when she was most vulnerable and in need of a caring touch. With a frown, he reached over to trace a gentle finger along the curve of her cheek.

"I didn't plan for this to happen, Tess," he said softly, his gaze locked on hers.

"Me, neither."

"Should I apologize?"

"Are you sorry?"

He studied her for a moment, then slowly shook his head. "No."

"Me, neither."

His frown disappeared then, and he somehow managed to dredge up a shaky smile. "In case you haven't figured it out, I wasn't pretending tonight when I implied to your ex that I was attracted to you."

Her face grew warm, and a feeling of elation and hope surged through her. "I just hope you're not disappointed. I haven't done this for a long time," she said tentatively.

Mitch chuckled, and Tess loved the intimate sound of the laughter rumbling deep in his chest. "Let's just say that I'm glad you're out of practice, because I'm not sure I could be responsible for my actions if you were any more responsive."

His tone was teasing, but Tess had a feeling he was more than half-serious. "I guess if…if we believe everything we read, at this point you should swing me up into your arms and…and…" She tried to tease, too, but her voice trailed off.

His eyes darkened and his intense gaze probed

hers. His voice no longer held even a pretense of teasing. "Would you like that, Tess?"

Tess looked at him steadily, her heart banging against her rib cage. "Yes," she whispered, the ardent light in her eyes confirming the honesty of her answer. "But I don't believe in casual intimacy. I think it cheapens what can otherwise be a beautiful emotional and spiritual experience."

His gaze never left hers, and after a beat of silence he spoke, his voice husky. "I feel the same way." He stroked her cheek tenderly with a whisper touch. "Besides, there's a lot we don't know about each other, Tess. And rushing into intimacy is never wise. Both of us still have issues we're dealing with. Time is on our side."

She looked at him wonderingly. "You continue to amaze me, Mr. Jackson."

"Why is that?"

"Patience isn't a virtue I've seen very often in men."

He grinned. "Well, I must admit it goes against all my instincts in this situation."

"Then I admire your self-control even more."

He chuckled and touched the tip of her nose with his index finger. "Then let me tell you, pretty lady, that you are one serious test of a man's self-control. So I'd better say good-night. Right now. Besides, you need your sleep." He looped his hands around her waist and pulled her close once again. "But how about one more good-night kiss first?"

Tess put her arms around his neck and tilted her head back to gaze up at him. "I want you to know that this has been the best night I've had in years, Mitch,'' she said softly. ''Thank you.''

His lazy smile was warm and very, very appealing. ''Trust me, Tess. It's been my pleasure.''

And as his lips closed over hers, making it clear that it was, indeed, his pleasure, Tess felt her heart sing. And for the first time in a very long while, she let herself believe, for just a moment, in happy endings.

''Are you going to tell Bruce that you ran into your ex?''

Tess glanced at Mitch. They were almost at the farm, and he looked as tired as she felt. Clearly, neither had slept well after their emotional encounter the evening before. Even now, the very thought of their kisses made Tess's nerve endings tingle. Her gaze drifted to Mitch's hands on the wheel, and as she recalled his touch a shudder of delight ran through her. But she needed to get her mind on something else, and Mitch had given her the perfect opening.

''I don't see any reason to. He made it pretty clear that he didn't have any intention of seeing Bruce while he was in town, and by now he's probably gone. I'm not sure it would serve any purpose, except to hurt Bruce. What do you think?''

Mitch nodded. ''I agree. When did Bruce last see his father?''

Tess frowned thoughtfully. ''Let's see…he moved to Washington right after the divorce. He did stop in once or twice when he was in Jeff City on business, but it's probably been…two or three years ago, I guess.''

"And he never calls?"

"Sometimes on Christmas."

A muscle in Mitch's jaw twitched. "How does Bruce feel about him?"

Tess frowned. "He doesn't talk about him at all anymore. I've tried to broach the subject a few times, thinking maybe it would be better if we did talk through his feelings, but he never responds. I know the hurt is still there, though. And it's had a big effect on his self-image. That feeling of being unwanted, of being unworthy, can have a lasting impact on an impressionable child."

He sent another quick glance her way. "And on a sensitive woman."

"Yes," she said quietly, turning to look at the passing countryside. "But at least an adult is a bit better equipped to cope. And I had my faith to sustain me. Adolescents often don't."

Mitch took one hand off the wheel and reached over to enfold her cold fingers in his warm clasp. "I know that Peter did a number on you both, Tess," he said gently. "But I hope by now you realize that the problem in your marriage was due to a lack on his part, not yours. No man in his right mind would do anything to jeopardize a relationship with a woman like you."

Warm color suffused her face. "Thank you for saying that."

"I'm saying it because it's true. You are a kind, intelligent, courageous, beautiful, appealing woman, Tess. I think I made that pretty clear last night."

Her color deepened. "You did. I just wish we could find a way to get through to Bruce, make him feel better about himself. I try, but it's hard to erase Peter's influence.''

Mitch frowned. "I'm not sure that's even possible. None of us can escape the past. But maybe, in time, with enough love and understanding, Bruce will come to recognize Peter for what he is—a selfish, self-centered man who never deserved to have a wife and son. And to recognize that no one man can validate his worth, even if that man happens to be his biological father.''

Tess sighed. "I hope so, Mitch. I do feel good about the progress he's made in the last few weeks—thanks to you.''

"Now, if only he could stop seeing me as the enemy,'' Mitch said ruefully.

"I think it's coming.''

"Maybe. In any case, I agree with you about the changes in him. He seems like a different kid now. He's enthusiastic about working on the sets for the school play, and he seems to be hanging out with a safer crowd. His teachers tell me his schoolwork is improving, too.''

"Let's just hope it continues.''

Mitch glanced over at her and flashed a smile. "I think it will. Especially if we work on it together.''

As he turned back to the road, Tess studied his profile. *Together* was a beautiful word, she realized. It spoke of sharing and caring and mutual support. Of partnership and companionship. Things that had long been absent from her life.

Tess didn't really know where she and Mitch were headed. Last night had left her filled with hope for the future. But life rarely kept its promises, at least in her experience. Great expectations often led to great disappointments.

She would be wise to consider *caution* her operative word, Tess told herself firmly. She needed to move carefully and thoughtfully and make no decisions without weighing all the pros and cons. That rational approach would be her life vest, keeping her afloat while she assessed her options.

There was only one little problem with that scenario, Tess realized with a sigh as she glanced at Mitch's strong profile, his capable and sensitive hands, the firm lines of his well-toned body.

When it came to Mitch, she was sinking fast.

# Chapter Eleven

"Hey, Uncle Ray, who's this?"

Bruce held up a dusty, framed photograph retrieved from a box of memorabilia that the older man was sorting through in his bedroom.

Uncle Ray peered at the faded color print, a studio portrait of a youngster with an impish grin and a sprinkling of freckles across his nose. "Land," he said softly. "I haven't seen that in years."

He reached out, and the teenager handed him the photo. "Was that your son?" Bruce asked cautiously.

Uncle Ray slowly shook his head. "No." He sat down wearily on the edge of the bed, still studying the photo. "But he was a special boy, too."

Bruce joined him. "Who was he?"

"So here's where you two are hiding! Tess and I are starving. Isn't it about time for—" Mitch's voice stopped abruptly and he froze in the doorway, his gaze riveted on the framed picture in Uncle Ray's hands. The color drained from his face and a bolt of white-hot pain zigzagged across his eyes.

Uncle Ray gave him a worried look. "We found this in my closet, Mitch," he said gently. "It must have been there for a long time. What with selling the land and all, it kind of got me in the mood to clean things out. Bruce has been helping me. We just came across this a minute ago."

Mitch drew in a harsh, ragged breath, then slowly walked over to the bed and held out an unsteady hand. Uncle Ray silently passed the framed picture to him, and for a long moment Mitch simply stared down at it, his lips a grim, unsmiling line. Finally, as if he couldn't bear to look at it any longer, he thrust the photograph back toward Uncle Ray. "Why did you keep it?" he asked harshly.

"I thought you might want it someday, son." The older man's voice was still gentle.

"Why? It only reminds me of…" His voice broke, and he sucked in a deep breath. When he spoke again, his voice was cold. "I never want to see it again, Uncle Ray. And I'd appreciate it if you'd get rid of it. Lunch will be ready in a few minutes."

With that, he turned stiffly and strode out of the room.

After a few beats of silence Bruce looked at the older man in disgust. "Boy, he sure can be a jerk sometimes. He was really mean to you, and all because of some dumb picture."

Uncle Ray turned to him. For the first time in their acquaintance, Bruce detected disapproval in the older man's gaze. "Sometimes people have reasons for the way they act," he said tersely. "You'll find that out as you get older.'' Then he stood and moved to his bureau, where he carefully stowed the picture that had caused such contention. "Let's go eat," Uncle Ray said shortly, leaving Bruce to follow at his own pace.

Bruce stared after him. Adults could be so weird sometimes! All that fuss about some old picture. And now he was more curious than ever about the identity of the mystery boy.

But he was pretty sure he wasn't going to find out today.

Though Tess had sensed Mitch's distraction for much of the afternoon, he'd certainly been single-minded in his determination to get her alone before they all retired for the night. And after a lingering good-night kiss, stolen surreptitiously out of sight and sound of Bruce and Uncle Ray, it had taken her a long time to get to sleep. But eventually she had fallen into a deep, sound slumber that was filled with the kinds of pleasant dreams she wished would go on and on forever.

Which was why she fought so hard to block the odd, unidentifiable noise that kept intruding on her subconscious, nudging her awake. It was a valiant but ultimately unsuccessful effort. With an irritated frown she opened her eyes and stared sleepily at the dark-ened ceiling of Uncle Ray's guest room.

Now, of course, all was silent. Only the distant whinny of a horse broke the stillness. But something had awakened her, she thought, her frown deepening.

And then she heard it. A muffled cry. Hoarse with pain, laced with anguish. A cry of such raw desolation and suffering that she became instantly and fully awake. It took her only a moment to pinpoint the location—the other side of the wall. The den. Where Mitch was sleeping.

Without even stopping to don a robe or slippers, she threw back the covers and swung her feet to the floor, panic rising within her. The sounds she was hearing were barely human, and they clawed at her insides. Something was very, very wrong.

Tess paused for only a brief moment at the den door. Now she could hear thrashing, and the guttural sounds of pain were louder. When her knock produced no response, she took a deep breath and opened the door.

In the dim moonlight filtering through the open window, Tess realized immediately that Mitch was having a nightmare. The bed linens were in disarray, his arms were flailing about, his face was contorted with pain and every muscle was tense. A sheen of sweat covered his torso, and his chest heaved with labored breathing.

Without hesitating, Tess moved toward him and dropped to one knee on the bed. She leaned over and took his shoulders in a firm grip, shaking gently at first, then harder when her initial efforts produced no results.

"Mitch. Mitch! Wake up!" she said urgently.

Neither her words nor her touch seemed to penetrate his consciousness. In fact, his thrashing intensified, and Tess found it difficult to maintain her hold on him. She'd always been aware of Mitch's strength, but now she had a firsthand demonstration of the dangerous power in his coiled muscles. She suddenly realized that in his frenzied state he could hurt not only her, but himself.

She also realized that she was in over her head. Mitch was too strong for her to restrain, and she couldn't rouse him short of shouting, which would only frighten Uncle Ray and Bruce. As she wrestled with the dilemma, Mitch suddenly reached out and grabbed her, his grip like a steel vise as his fingers bit into the tender flesh of her upper arms. She gasped in pain, and this time when she spoke, there was fear in her voice. And it was the fear that finally seemed to penetrate his cloud of horror. His eyelids fluttered open and he stared at her, disoriented and confused.

"It's okay, Mitch," Tess reassured him shakily, speaking deliberately and clearly. "You were just having a nightmare. You're all right."

Slowly the lines of strain in his face eased, and gradually his grip on her arms loosened. He closed his eyes and sucked in a deep breath, then reached out and pulled her close, holding her fiercely against his chest. She could feel the tremors running through him, and she murmured soothingly as she would to a frightened child.

"It's all right, Mitch. It's over. I'm here. Just relax. It was only a bad dream. It's not real."

Slowly she began to feel the tension in his coiled muscles ease. She gently stroked his face until the wild thudding of his heart gradually subsided. When at last he drew a shuddering breath and made a move to sit up, Tess started to stand.

"Stay. Please. Just for a few minutes," he said hoarsely, reaching out a hand to restrain her.

His plea was filled with raw need, and as she stared

into his haggard face a wave of tenderness washed over her. She inched closer until she was sitting beside him, then reached over to lay her hand on his cheek. He covered it with his own. "Of course I'll stay," she said, her voice choked with emotion. "For as long as you need me."

Mitch took her hand and pressed it to his lips, his intense gaze riveted on hers. "That could be a very long time," he said, his voice still hoarse.

Tess stared at him, and her mouth went dry. He seemed to be talking about far more than recovering from a nightmare. And she'd meant far more than that with her statement as well, she realized. But now was not the time to go into that. Not when Mitch was still reeling from a visit to some private hell. "I'm glad I was here for you tonight," she said huskily.

"So am I. Usually I have to deal with that nightmare alone."

She frowned. "You've had it before?"

"Many times."

"Oh, Mitch!" Her voice was laced with compassion. "I'm sorry. It seemed horrible."

He grimaced. "Not as horrible as the reality."

The furrows in her brow deepened. "What do you mean?"

Mitch looked at her in the dim light. He was fast falling in love with Tess. To deny it would be foolish. And unless he had completely misread the situation, she felt the same way about him.

And now they were at a crossroads. If they were going to move forward, they had to be honest with each other. There could be no secrets between them, no fears. She'd taken a great risk yesterday by trusting him with a painful episode from her past, something she'd shared with no one. She'd bared her soul by revealing her humiliation and pain at Peter's infidelity. Turnabout was only fair play—even if there was a good chance she might want nothing more to do with him when she heard what he had done. Yet it was a risk he had to take eventually. And putting it off was the coward's way out. *Lord, please be with me,* he prayed silently. *Give me the courage to share this terrible secret. And please give Tess the strength to bear it without turning away from me.*

At last Mitch drew a deep breath and laced his fingers with hers, his gaze once more locked on hers. "I mean the nightmare really happened, Tess. Six years ago."

She looked into his eyes, still shadowed with horror, and a cold knot of fear formed in her stomach. An experience that had the power to completely unnerve a strong, capable man like Mitch, to haunt his dreams for years, to leave him physically and mentally shaken was an experience she wasn't sure she wanted to hear about. And yet Mitch seemed to be encouraging her to ask about it.

"Do…do you want to tell me about it?" she asked hesitantly.

His gaze held hers prisoner, and though she couldn't clearly read the expression in his eyes in the dim light, she could sense he was assessing her question and debating his response. Several long seconds ticked by before he slowly spoke. "I've only talked about this to one person, Tess."

"Uncle Ray." It was more statement than question. The bond between the two men was almost tangible.

He nodded. "We've shared a lot. And I *owe* him a lot. In fact, he saved my life six years ago." Again he hesitated, and when he spoke it was clear he was carefully choosing his words. "You remember last night, when you said that what you had to tell me wasn't pretty? Well, this is even less pretty."

Tess swallowed. "I've seen ugly, Mitch."

"Not like this."

She gripped his hand more tightly. "I can handle it," she replied with more assurance than she felt.

He angled his body toward hers and took her free hand in his, studying her eyes once again, his gaze compelling and touched with fear. "I don't want to lose you over this, Tess."

The knot in her stomach tightened at the raw honesty of his statement. He was warning her that she was about to hear something bad. Very bad. So bad that he was afraid she would walk away afterward. But Tess couldn't imagine Mitch doing something terrible enough to change her feelings for him. Yet his fear was very real. And Mitch wasn't a man who frightened easily. Which only made *her* afraid. And uncertain.

Tess realized he was waiting for a response, and so she also spoke honestly, from her heart. "I don't want to lose you, either, Mitch," she whispered, her voice catching.

He almost lost his courage then. She hadn't said, "I'll stick by you, no matter what." But then, what did he expect? Their relationship was still too new, too tenuous, to breed promises. He probably should have waited to bring this up, until they were on more solid footing. But it was too late now for second thoughts. He'd gone too far to back out.

Several long moments of silence passed, and then Mitch took a deep, steadying breath. Telling his story to Uncle Ray had been hard. Yet he'd known the older man would offer support, even if he didn't approve of Mitch's behavior. But this was even harder. Because there was no such guarantee with Tess. He could only hope and trust that she would find it in her heart to still care for him despite what he had done.

"I told you once that when I was a cop, my job always came first," he said slowly, his voice not quite steady. "And because of that, I wasn't always the best husband. What I didn't tell you was that I also wasn't the best...father."

He stopped, giving Tess a moment to digest this revelation. He watched the rapid succession of emotions flash across her face as she processed this new information. Confusion. Shock. Uncertainty.

"You have a child?" She said it wonderingly, as if her ears were playing tricks on her.

"No. I *had* a child," he corrected her.

She frowned and gave a slight shake of her head. "Had?"

"I had a son, Tess. His name was..." He paused and tried to swallow past the lump in his throat. "David. He died when he was thirteen."

A mask of shock slipped over her face. "Oh, Mitch!" she breathed. "I'm so sorry."

"That's not the worst of it."

Tess couldn't even *imagine* anything worse than losing a child. "What do you mean?"

"He didn't have to die."

They were coming to the nightmare part of the story. Tess could sense it. She squeezed his hand, but remained silent, waiting for him to continue.

"Do you remember you asked me once how I know so much about kids?" he asked.

She nodded.

"Well, I learned the hard way. And too late to save my own son." He drew an unsteady breath, then let it out slowly. "When Dana died, I was beside myself with grief. And guilt. I realized how unfair I'd been to her by always putting my job first. I gave what I thought was enough to her and David, and I loved them both in my own way, but it was a love that was secondary to my commitment to my job. And I can't even claim that it was a noble commitment. Sure, I liked seeing justice done. But what I enjoyed most was the thrill of the chase and the excitement.

"When Dana died, I couldn't think straight. Even though I dealt with life-and-death situations every day, it had never even occurred to me that my own life could be affected by an untimely death. I just figured that the three of us had plenty of time to be a family, and that I'd get around to it eventually. Then reality hit me in the face."

He paused, and a flash of pain seared across his eyes. "You'd think that an experience like that would make me step back and take stock of my priorities. To back off the job and spend more time with the people I loved—particularly my son. Instead, I immersed myself even more deeply in my work. Not because of the excitement anymore. At least I'd gotten past that. But because it was an escape. I simply couldn't deal with my loss, and I figured if I kept myself busy enough I wouldn't have time to think about it.

"And that was a huge mistake. Because David needed me during those months. Desperately. He'd lost his mother, and he needed my emotional support. But I was so caught up in my own grief, I was oblivious to his. For all intents and purposes, I was lost to him, too. My mother, who was a widow, moved in with us and she tried her best to help David, but he needed me. She told me that, many times, but I simply didn't get the message.

"That's when David started slipping away, finding his own way to deal with his grief. Namely, drugs. I had no clue what was happening—that's how out of touch I was with my own son." He paused and gave a brief, bitter laugh, his mouth twisting in irony. "Me, the hotshot cop who dealt with dealers and addicts every day, didn't even recognize the signs in my own son. Until the night of…of the nightmare."

Mitch closed his eyes, and a spasm of pain crossed his face. When he spoke again, his voice was raw, his words choppy. "One night my partner and I were sent to check out a deserted warehouse. It was reportedly being used for drug deals. The minute I walked inside I sensed something was wrong. You develop that sixth sense after a while working as a cop. You have to, or you don't survive. My partner and I split up to check the place out. It was absolutely quiet inside. And dark. All I had was a flashlight. The place was littered with debris. There was so much trash that I almost missed…the shoe."

Mitch's grip had tightened painfully on her hand, but Tess remained silent, her gaze riveted on his face.

"I was sweeping the flashlight back and forth, and I went right over it. But something...something made me turn the light back on it. It was a sneaker. Next to some crates. And it was...attached to a leg."

Tess drew in a sharp breath, and her heart began to beat rapidly. Mitch continued to speak, but it was almost as if he didn't realize she was there anymore. He was staring past her, his gaze focused not on this safe, cozy room, but on a dark warehouse that held unspeakable horror.

"I had this...this awful feeling of dread," he said in a choked voice. "I moved the light up the body. Slowly. Everything suddenly seemed to be happening in slow motion. But finally I got to the face, and it was...it was..." His voice broke on a sob and his head dropped forward. "Dear God! I can never forget that moment! He was my only s-son and I f-failed him. He d-died because of m-me."

The knot in Tess's stomach tightened convulsively, and for a moment her lungs seemed to stop working. The horror of it was almost too great to imagine. How could a parent survive such a cruel twist of fate? No wonder Mitch was still having nightmares about it six years after the fact. Especially since he held himself responsible for his son's death.

Tess looked at Mitch's bowed head. His shoulders were heaving, and though his tears were silent, they were no less wrenching. Tess knew intuitively that Mitch rarely, if ever, cried. And that when and if he did, it was in solitude. He was the kind of man people leaned on, the kind of man people looked to for strength. And he knew that. And lived up to those expectations. But once in a very great while that burden was too great to bear, too heavy for even the strongest shoulders. And this was one of those moments.

Tess didn't have to reassess her feelings for Mitch. If anything, his confession made her care for him more, not less. Yes, he had made mistakes. Bad ones. But he had learned from them. Had transformed his life because of them. And while he couldn't bring back his son, he had given the youngster's death some meaning by subsequently devoting his own life to helping other troubled teens avoid that same tragic end.

Tess's heart contracted with tenderness for this special man who had suffered such loss. She'd always sensed that his character had been forged in fire, and now her intuition had been verified. Despite his own self-deprecating remarks, Tess knew in her heart that Mitch had always been a good man. But it was the trials he'd gone through that had made him a *great* one. A man worthy of admiration. Of respect. And of love.

Love. Tess replayed that word in her mind, savoring the sound of it. Until Mitch came along, she had believed that love wasn't in the cards for her. But he had changed all that. He'd made her feel young and beautiful and desirable. And he'd made her believe in happy endings again. He'd given her hope that her tomorrows need not be as lonely as her yesterdays. He'd opened the door to a whole new world of possibilities. And along the way, she'd fallen in love with him.

Hot tears rose to her eyes as her heart overflowed with love and compassion for this wonderful man who gave and gave without asking anything in return. Who was capable of dealing with pain alone. But who didn't need to anymore.

Tess reached out to him then, scooting closer until she could wrap her arms around his broad shoulders. His arms went around her involuntarily, and he buried his face in her neck, clinging to her with a desperation that said more eloquently than words how much he needed her, how much he cared for her, how much he trusted her.

For several long moments they held each other, until Mitch at last backed off slightly to stare down at her. He touched her face gently, reverently, as if to reassure himself that she really was there. "You didn't bolt."

"Did you think I would?"

"I wouldn't have blamed you if you had."

"You're harder on yourself than anyone else would be."

"I'm honest. If I'd been there for David in his grief, he might still be alive."

"You were dealing with your own grief, Mitch. You weren't thinking clearly."

"That's no excuse," he said harshly. "I neglected David. And he died. Period."

"A lot of kids get involved with drugs even when they have attentive parents."

"Yeah. But I was never an attentive parent even before Dana's death. I was always too busy with my job. And both she and David suffered."

"Would you do the same thing today?"

He frowned and gave her a startled look. "Of course not."

"Because you learned and you grew and you moved on. You devoted yourself to helping kids, and you're making a difference in a lot of lives. Like Bruce's. And you do it with absolute dedication and selflessness. I suspect you're a different man today than you were six years ago, Mitch."

He stared at her. "That's what Uncle Ray said."

"He's a very wise man. You should listen to him."

"He also said I shouldn't spend the rest of my life alone. And lonely."

Tess stared at him silently in the dim light, suddenly finding it difficult to breathe. "And what did you say?"

He drew a deep breath. "That I was scared. Of messing things up. Making the same mistakes. Hurting the people I love. Just like before. But he didn't buy it. He said I'd changed, and that it was time to move on." Mitch gently caressed her face, and she quivered under his touch. "I think maybe he's right," he whispered hoarsely.

Tess felt as if her heart was going to burst, it was so filled with joy and elation and hope. "Oh, Mitch!" she said in a choked voice.

"I love you, Tess."

"I love you, too."

"I didn't plan for this to happen, you know."

"Neither did I."

"Are you sorry?"

She smiled up at him, and though the light was dim, there was no mistaking the happiness in her eyes. "Do I look sorry?"

One corner of his mouth rose in amusement. "Hardly."

"Are you...sorry?"

His smile disappeared. "No. But I *am* scared."

"Join the crowd."

He ran his hand around the back of her neck, under her hair, and caressed her nape. "Maybe cautious is a better word," he said softly. "Because when I'm with you, I'm not scared at all. It's only when we're apart that I have doubts."

"I feel the same way," she breathed.

"Then there's only one solution. We have to spend as much time together as possible."

"I like the sound of that. Except..." Her eyes grew troubled, and though her instinct was to throw caution to the wind and simply go with the flow, her maternal instinct was too strong to allow her that luxury.

"Except what?" he prompted gently, caressing her nape with his thumb.

She swallowed, trying to hold on to rational thought for at least another few seconds. "Except I have to think of Bruce, too. And what's best for him."

"And?"

"And you two haven't exactly...I mean, I'd want anyone I was going to—" She cut herself off. She'd almost said "marry," but she suddenly realized that Mitch hadn't used that word. "Anyone I was going to be involved with to have a good relationship with him."

"I understand that, Tess. He's your first responsibility. Trust me, I respect that. And I like Bruce. He's a great kid with great potential. And he and I are making progress. How about if we just put this in the

Lord's hands, give it a little time and see how things go?"

Her eyes misted. "You're willing to do that?"

He smiled gently. "If that's what it takes to put your mind at ease."

She shook her head unbelievingly. "How did I ever find you?"

"I've been asking myself that same question about you for quite a while now."

She searched his eyes, and the love she saw made her throat tighten with emotion. She reached up and touched his face, and suddenly he pulled her even closer, until she was again pressed tightly against him. She clung to him for a long moment, then drew a shuddering breath and gazed up at him.

"I should leave," she whispered tremulously.

His eyes deepened in color, and he swallowed convulsively. "In a minute," he replied hoarsely.

And then his lips came down on hers, as greedy, hungry and demanding as her own. It was a kiss filled with urgency and need and long-suppressed desires, a kiss that ignited, that consumed, that possessed, that promised. And though they both knew that there were still challenges ahead, for just this moment they forgot the world. As his hands pressed her closer, Tess was lost to everything but his touch. Just as he was lost to everything but the feel of her soft curves and her sweet lips on his.

In fact, they were so lost that neither saw the shadow of the lanky teenager slide across the hall wall and disappear into the darkness.

# Chapter Twelve

"Bruce! What on earth happened?"

Tess crossed the kitchen in two swift strides and took Bruce's chin in her hand, tilting his head toward the light coming from the window to examine a brand-new black eye that was discoloring rapidly.

"Nothing," he replied, trying to pull away.

"This is not nothing," she said sharply, leading him toward a kitchen chair. "Sit here while I get some ice."

"I don't need any ice."

"Sit," she repeated sternly.

He complied without further argument, and she turned away to prepare a makeshift ice bag out of a dish towel. Her heart was pounding, and she had to force herself to take several long, slow breaths as anger, concern and disappointment all clamored for top billing. Anger because Bruce appeared to once again be in trouble. Concern about his physical condition. And disappointment because things had been going so well. But when she turned back to her son and looked again at the angry purple and red of his injured eye, her heart contracted and concern won hands down.

She walked over to him and placed the bag carefully against his bruised skin, touching his shoulder comfortingly when he flinched. "I'm sorry," she said gently. "I know it hurts. But this will keep the swelling down. Hold it in place, okay?"

"Yeah."

She sank into the chair next to him and reached out to cover his free hand with her own, noting with a jolt that his knuckles were bruised and scraped. "Oh, Bruce!" she said in dismay, rising as she spoke. "I'll get some antiseptic."

"It's okay, Mom."

She ignored him and headed for the medicine cabinet in the bathroom, suddenly wondering as she rummaged among the first-aid items if he might have other, less visible injuries. She hurried back, and though she tried to remain calm, there was a note of panic in her voice when she spoke. "Are you hurt anywhere else?"

"No."

"Bruce."

For the first time, he met her gaze. "No, Mom," he said firmly. "This is it."

She searched his eyes, but saw only honesty. With a sigh, she nodded and set to work with the antiseptic. "Okay. Do you want to tell me what happened?"

"I got in a fight."

"I figured that. What about?"

Her question was met with silence, and she looked over at him. "Well?"

He shifted uncomfortably, and his gaze slid away. "Nothing."

She expelled a long, frustrated sigh. "Come on, Bruce. Fights don't happen because of nothing. Does Mr. Jackson know about this?"

He gave her a defiant look. "No. If he did, don't you think he'd have called you by now?"

She frowned. "What do you mean?"

"You guys tell each other everything."

Her frown deepened. "Why do you say that?"

He shrugged. "You hang around together a lot."

"We're friends."

"Yeah, well…the guys say you're more than that."

She looked startled. "What?"

His gaze skittered away. "They say you're sleeping together."

Bright spots of anger began to burn in her cheeks. "What guys are these?"

"The guys I used to hang around with."

The gang. It figured. "And what did *you* say?"

"I told them they were full of cr…that they were wrong."

Suddenly the light began to dawn. "Is that how you got the black eye?" she asked slowly.

"Yeah. I was just going to ignore them and walk away, but they started shoving me around."

Tess's stomach clenched. "How many of them were there?"

"Three. But only two of them hit me."

Anger bubbled to the surface again—and with it, fear. If they'd beaten up on Bruce once, they could do it again. And next time he might not escape with only a black eye. Abruptly she rose and headed for the phone.

"What are you doing?" Bruce asked in alarm.

"Calling Mitch. Those hoodlums need to be reported."

"Mom! Don't do that! This didn't happen at school. Besides, they won't bother me again."

She paused in midstride and turned to him. "Why not?"

"Because they look worse than I do."

She stared at him, then slowly walked back to the table and sank into her chair. She knew he'd been going to the gym for the past few weeks, knew that he'd filled out and was developing muscles. But she hadn't realized he was so capable of taking care of himself.

"Joe's been helping me with my workouts. And he showed me some tricks," Bruce added, confirming her conclusion.

There was a touch of pride in his voice, and Tess couldn't blame him. She didn't condone fighting, but she was relieved to know he could defend himself if necessary. And the ability to deal with a situation like today's was obviously a boost to his self-esteem. Besides, he'd done nothing wrong. He hadn't started the fight. He'd just taken care of himself when things started getting rough.

"I think you handled this in exactly the right way, Bruce," she said slowly. "I'm proud of you. I'm just sorry they said those things to you about me."

He shifted uncomfortably, and when he spoke he sounded suddenly like a little boy, uncertain and afraid and desperately in need of reassurance. "They aren't true, are they, Mom?" he asked in a small voice.

She stared at him. "Of course not!"

He flushed and looked away. "Sorry. I didn't think so, but...well, you and Mr. Jackson seem pretty... close. Even the guys noticed."

Tess took a deep breath and then reached out to hold his bruised hand, forcing him to look at her again. She needed to be honest, and to say this just the right way, so she chose her words carefully. "We are, Bruce. We're very close. In fact, we've fallen in love. Mitch is a very special man, and I feel blessed that he's part of our life. But just because we're in love doesn't mean we're sleeping together. That would go against everything I believe, everything our faith teaches. Sleeping together, making love, only means something when it's done in the context of a long-term commitment. Of marriage. Knowing that your partner will be with you for always, through the good times and the bad times, is what gives love-making its deepest meaning. Mitch feels the same way."

"So are you going to marry him, then?"

She took a deep breath and once again struggled to find the right words. "First of all, he hasn't asked me to yet. And second, a lot depends on you. You are my first and most important commitment," she said fervently, her gaze locked on his. "I would never do anything that wasn't in your best interest. I happen to think that having Mitch in your life *is* in your best interest, and I hope you will feel the same way in time. Because I have room in my life—and my heart—for both of you. Loving Mitch takes nothing away from the special relationship that we have. Do you understand that?''

There was silence for a moment, and then he slowly nodded. ''Yeah.''

He sounded sincere, and relief surged through Tess. ''So tell me how you feel about Mitch.''

Bruce shrugged. ''He's okay, I guess. He's not as bad as I thought at first.''

Tess considered extolling Mitch's virtues, pointing out all the wonderful things he'd done for Bruce and for her. The evidence was pretty compelling. But she refrained. Bruce needed to come to those conclusions himself. And he would, she was sure, given time.

Mitch was willing to wait, so that wasn't a problem.

The problem was her. Because after years of being alone, she was suddenly tired of waiting.

''Tess? Jenny Stevenson.''

Tess frowned at the phone. Why in the world would Peter's sister be calling her?

''Tess? Are you there?''

''Yes. Hello, Jenny. Sorry. I was just surprised.''

''I'm sure you were. We haven't talked in years. And I wouldn't have bothered you now, except I thought you might want to know, for Bruce's sake.'' The woman's voice broke on the last word, and Tess heard her take a deep breath as she struggled to regain her composure. ''Peter had a massive heart attack yesterday. He died this morning.''

Tess stared at the phone. Peter dead at age forty-two? Of a heart attack? He'd never been sick a day in his life!

"Tess?"

"Yes. I—I'm here. I'm just so…shocked."

"We all feel the same way. The funeral will be in Washington on Saturday, and I thought maybe Bruce might like to come."

"Thanks for letting me know. I'll…I'll talk with him about it."

"Let me give you the information. Do you have a piece of paper handy?"

She reached for a notepad. "Yes. Go ahead."

As Tess jotted down the details, her mind was reeling. Even after she'd expressed her polite condolences and said goodbye, she was still too stunned to fully absorb the news. She sat there unmoving as the minutes ticked by, thinking about the man who had been her husband, and about the sham of their marriage. About his selfishness and unfaithfulness. About the way he'd hurt his only son. His legacy to both of them had been only pain and tattered self-esteem.

Tess supposed she should feel some hint of sadness at his death. Some remorse.

But, God forgive her, all she felt was relief. Because now he could never hurt them again.

"Hey, Mom, I'm home!"

Tess's heart began to pound and she carefully set the paring knife on the counter. She didn't know how Bruce was going to react to the news about Peter. He'd talked so little about his father through the years, guarded his feelings so closely, that she had no idea how he felt about him now. For that reason, she had decided to leave the decision to him about whether to attend the funeral. If he needed to go, for closure, she would see that he got there. But she would also fully support him if he decided to stay in St. Louis.

She turned as he came into the kitchen and threw his books onto the table, noting with relief that the black and blue of his eye had faded dramatically in the week since the fight.

"What's for dinner?" he asked.

"Stir-fry. How was school?"

"Okay."

"And the play?"

"Scenery's almost done. But I'll probably have to stay late again tomorrow to help finish up." He reached over and snatched a piece of raw carrot from the pile of crisp vegetables. "I'm gonna check my e-mail before dinner. Uncle Ray's supposed to send me some stuff about putting up fences before I go out there Saturday."

He started to turn away, but Tess reached out a hand to restrain him. "Bruce, before you go I need to talk with you for a minute."

At the serious tone of her voice he turned back to her with a worried look. "What's wrong?"

"Let's sit down for a minute, okay?"

"You aren't sick again, are you?"

He followed her to the table but stood hovering over her anxiously, his face tense.

"No, honey, I'm fine. Come on, sit down."

"Is something wrong with Uncle Ray?" A note of panic crept into his voice.

"As far as I know, he's fine, too. It's your...your dad, Bruce."

Bruce frowned and slowly sat down. "What about him?" he asked cautiously.

"He had a heart attack yesterday. He died this morning."

Bruce's face grew a shade paler, and his eyes shuttered. Tess couldn't even begin to gauge his reaction. But his hand was ice-cold when she reached for it. She waited for several moments, but when he made no comment, she continued.

"Peter's sister, your aunt Jenny, called about half an hour ago. She gave me all the information on the funeral. It's going to be on Saturday, in Washington. You can go if you'd like to, Bruce."

He frowned. "Do I have to?"

"No. It's completely up to you. I just want you to know that you *can* go if that's what you want to do."

"You aren't going, are you?"

"Not to the funeral. But I'll go to Washington with you and make sure you get to the service if you decide to go."

Bruce stared down at the table. "Do you think I *should* go, Mom?"

Tess leaned closer and put her arm around his shoulders. "You don't owe your father anything, Bruce," she said quietly. "Don't go because you think you're supposed to. Only go if you want to. And either way is fine with me."

He was silent for a moment. "Can I think about it tonight?"

"Of course."

Bruce sighed. "He wasn't much of a father."

Tess felt her throat constrict. That was the closest Bruce had ever come to revealing his feelings about the man who had been a father in name only. "No, honey. He wasn't. It just wasn't a role he was cut out to play."

"Yeah." He leaned over and gave her a quick bear hug. "But you're a great mom." When he drew back, his eyes were suspiciously moist, and he swiped at them with the back of his hand as he stood. "I think I'll check my e-mail now."

Before Tess could respond, he grabbed his books and headed for his room. She watched him disappear down the hall, too choked up to speak. Peter might not have been much of a father. But he had certainly fathered a wonderful son.

"Well now, I think it's about time for lunch." Uncle Ray mopped his brow and squinted at his watch, shading it from the sun. "Putting up fences sure can build up an appetite. You boys hungry yet?"

"I could use some food," Mitch replied. "How about you, Bruce?"

"Yeah. I guess so," the teenager concurred. "Do you need some help, Uncle Ray?"

"Nope. Got all the sandwich fixings in the refrigerator. Only take me a few minutes to whip everything up. I'll ring the bell when it's ready."

For a moment they watched the older man make his way back toward the house, and then Bruce reached for the posthole digger and went back to work.

Mitch did the same, keeping a surreptitious eye on the teenager. Bruce had been unusually subdued this

morning—which wasn't surprising, considering his
father was being buried even as they worked. The
funeral was clearly on his mind, though he hadn't
mentioned it. Tess had warned Mitch about Bruce's
reticence. Other than telling her he'd decided not to
go to the funeral, he hadn't spoken about the subject.
He was making a valiant effort to ignore the whole
thing, pretend it didn't matter. But Mitch could sense
the tension in the boy. His movements were stiff, and
there was an unnatural tautness to his face. Mitch had
tried to raise the subject of the funeral during the
drive to the farm, only to have his efforts rebuffed.
But the boy was clearly hurting, so Mitch decided to
make another attempt using a different approach.

"I wonder if Uncle Ray will miss having the
farm," he said, keeping his tone conversational. "He
hasn't said much about it."

At first Mitch thought Bruce was going to ignore
the comment. But after a few moments he spoke. "He
has to me."

"Is that right? So what do you think?"

Bruce kept digging. "I don't think he'll miss the
work. And he kept some land, so he can still have a
garden. I think he's happy. At least, he seems like he
is whenever we talk about it."

"You two seem to talk a lot."

"Yeah. We e-mail almost every day. He's a great
guy. It must be neat to have an uncle like that."

"It is. He's been almost like a father to me since
my own dad died ten years ago," Mitch said evenly,
keeping his tone casual.

There was silence for a few moments, and again

Mitch thought Bruce was going to shut down. But the boy surprised him. "Did you have a good dad?"

"Yes. He worked too hard. And he wasn't around as much as I would have liked. But he loved me. And he let me know it. In the end, that's all that matters."

"You were lucky." Bruce thrust the posthole digger into the ground and clamped it shut on the dark earth.

"Yes, I was."

Bruce withdrew the dirt and deposited it in a pile beside the hole, kicking a few wayward clumps back into place. "I guess Mom told you a lot about my dad."

"Some."

Bruce looked at him skeptically. "More than that, I bet."

"Enough," Mitch amended. "He didn't sound like the best dad—or husband."

"He wasn't," Bruce said tersely, his voice edged with anger. He thrust the digger into the ground again. "He hurt Mom real bad."

"I figured that. What about you?"

Bruce shrugged as he withdrew another digger of dirt. "He never wanted me around. That's pretty hard for a little kid."

Or a teenager, Mitch thought silently. "Even adults have a hard time dealing with rejection," he replied quietly.

"Yeah. I guess so." Bruce paused and wiped his forehead on his sleeve.

"How about some lemonade?" Mitch suggested.

"Sure."

Mitch filled two paper cups from the cooler Uncle

Ray had provided, then nodded toward a large rock a few yards away in the shade. "What do you say we take a break?"

"We'll be stopping for lunch in a few minutes."

Mitch smiled. "I don't think Uncle Ray will fire us if we cut out a few minutes early."

Mitch headed for the rock and settled down. Bruce followed more slowly and perched on the edge, his body tense, his eyes fixed on the distant field. It was quiet at the farm, the stillness broken only by the faint hum of a tractor and the birds twittering in the trees. There was silence between them for a minute or two, but finally Bruce sighed.

"I wish my dad had been more like Uncle Ray," he said, his tone subdued but intense. "I only met him a couple of months ago, but already I know I'd miss him real bad if…if anything happened to him. I never felt that way about my dad. He was never very nice to me. Or to Mom. It's real hard to…to love somebody like that, you know? Even though you're supposed to."

Mitch took a sip of his lemonade. *Lord, let me say the right thing,* he prayed silently, forming his words carefully. "You don't have to love him just because he was your biological dad, Bruce. That kind of love isn't something that's owed. It's something that's earned. And from what I know about your dad, he didn't earn your love. Or your mom's. And you know something? That was his loss. Because he could have had the love of two very special people if he'd just made an effort."

Bruce turned to look at him, and Mitch met his gaze directly. After a moment Bruce blinked and turned away. "He didn't think I was special," he said in a small voice. "He never wanted me."

"Then he was a fool. I would give anything to…to have a son like you." Mitch's own voice broke, and he suddenly found it difficult to swallow past the lump in his throat.

Bruce turned back to him, remembering the photo that Uncle Ray had so carefully placed in his dresser drawer, recalling the scene he'd witnessed—and the confession he'd overheard—the night of Mitch's nightmare. "That picture in Uncle Ray's room…the day you came in to call us for lunch. That boy was your son, wasn't he?" Bruce said slowly.

Mitch nodded.

"I'm sorry he died. He looked like a nice kid."

Mitch sucked in a deep breath, struggling to control his own emotions. "He was."

"You still miss him, don't you?"

"Yes."

"The same way Uncle Ray misses his son."

Again Mitch nodded.

"I know that they both died when they were pretty young, but they were kind of lucky in a way," Bruce said, his eyes suddenly old beyond his years.

Mitch frowned. "What do you mean?"

He shrugged. "They had fathers who cared. And who loved them. And who still think about them a long time after they're gone. If something had happened to me, my dad would never have even given it a second thought. He would have forgotten all about me by the next day."

Mitch's heart contracted, and he once more silently cursed the man who had come very close to ruining a young boy's life. But he couldn't deny what was obviously a true statement. So he didn't even try. "Maybe you should follow his lead, then."

Bruce sent him a puzzled look. "What do you mean?"

"Now that he's gone, forget about him. Recognize him for what he was—and what he wasn't—and move on with your life. You don't need your dad to validate your worth, Bruce. You never did. You're a smart, caring, talented young man. And if your dad failed to recognize how special you are, that's his fault, not yours."

Bruce's face grew slightly pink at Mitch's compliment, and he looked away. "It's not easy to forget," he said quietly.

A flash of pain flared in Mitch's eyes. "No, it's not. That's why it's important to have people around who love us and believe in us and stand by us when we have doubts."

"Like Mom."

"And your friends, too. Like Uncle Ray. And me."

Bruce looked at him, and for a moment their gazes connected and held. The boy's Adam's apple bobbed convulsively, and he took a deep breath. "I haven't been very friendly to you."

"Principals are used to that."

"I thought you were picking on me when I first came to the school."

"How about now?"

Bruce met his gaze steadily. "I guess I was wrong."

The clanging of the dinner bell suddenly broke the

stillness, and after a moment Mitch forced his lips into a smile. "Sounds like Uncle Ray's ready for us."

"Yeah. He's worse than Mom when you're late for a meal."

This time Mitch's grin was genuine. "Then we'd better hurry."

They stood, and Bruce shoved his hands into his pockets. But when he held back, Mitch turned to him questioningly.

"I don't think I ever said thanks for everything you've done for Mom and me," the boy said quietly.

Mitch put his hand on Bruce's shoulder. "You just did. And it was my pleasure."

He slung his arm around Bruce's shoulders, and as they made their way to the house, Mitch felt more at peace than he had in a very long while. Because for the first time he and Bruce had finally found some common ground. And in the process they'd forged a new bond.

# Chapter Thirteen

"I take it the news was good."

Mitch paused at Karen's desk and grinned. "Did you have a spy planted in the boardroom?"

"Didn't need one. Your face tells the story. Let me give you one word of advice—don't ever play poker."

"Don't worry. It's not my game."

"Good. So…the assistant-principal position was approved and you will now have some time to call your own. You should go out and celebrate."

Mitch reached into his pocket and fingered the square velvet case, anticipating his dinner with Tess. "I intend to."

"Not alone, I hope."

"Hardly."

"I didn't think so. Give Ms. Lockwood my best," Karen said breezily, turning back to her word processor.

Mitch stared at her. "How did you know?"

Karen sent him a smug look over her shoulder. "I have my ways."

Mitch shook his head. "I told you you missed your calling. Would you care to let me know how you found out I was seeing her?"

"Well, I usually don't reveal my sources," Karen said, pretending to give his request serious consideration before relenting. "But just this once I guess it couldn't hurt. My neighbor, a nice older woman, Mrs. Brown, was at the grocery store and ran into Ted Randall—you remember Ted, he used to do some of the groundskeeping work here—and he told her that he'd seen you going into a very nice restaurant the night you left here in the suit. He couldn't remember the name of it, but Mrs. Brown did, and I happen to know one of the hostesses there. Strangely enough, I crossed paths with her a couple of days later, and I asked if by chance she'd seen you at the restaurant. She knew what you looked like from that article in the paper when you won the award, because I'd called it to her attention and she thought you were a hunk. Well, turns out she did see you. And oddly enough, she recognized Tess Lockwood from some meeting she attended that Tess was covering for the paper. So she told me who you were with. Small world, isn't it?"

Mitch gave her a dazed look. "I think I'm sorry I asked."

Karen chuckled. "That's what my husband always says. So why don't you get out of here? For once in your life, leave before seven o'clock. The world won't end. And remember—thanks to the board, help is on the way."

"Not until next year," he reminded her.

She waved his caveat aside. "Be here before you know it. And school's almost out for this year, anyway. There's more to life than work, you know."

He thought of Tess, and his lips slowly curved upward. "Yeah. I know."

"Well, it's about time," she declared with a satisfied smile.

Mitch chuckled and shook his head. "Karen, you are priceless."

She sniffed. "Remember that when it comes time for raises."

Mitch was still chuckling as he entered his office and headed for his desk. All he had to do was put a few papers in his briefcase and he could be on his way.

Out of habit, he glanced at the phone, noting that the message light was on. Nothing new there. It always seemed to be on. He hesitated and glanced at his watch. The board meeting had run long, and Tess was expecting him in less than fifteen minutes. There was no way he'd be on time if he began checking his messages. And tonight was one night he did *not* want to be late, he reminded himself, reaching into his pocket again to finger the velvet box.

His expression grew tender and a smile stole over his face. He'd hinted to Tess that big things were up at school and he might have some news after the board meeting. So she was expecting a celebration dinner. But although the addition of an assistant principal was definitely worth celebrating, he had an entirely different kind of celebration in mind.

\* \* \*

"*That* was a fabulous dinner," Tess declared, leaning back with a sigh in the upholstered chair. "And so is this restaurant," she added, glancing around admiringly at the discreetly elegant decor.

"And how about the company?" Mitch teased with a smile.

Her gaze returned to his, and her own lips curved up. "Even better than the food and the setting," she assured him softly.

He reached for her hand and leaned closer. "I was hoping you'd say that."

Tess studied him for a moment in the candlelight. It still astounded her that this amazing man had come into her life. He was handsome, yes. But even more, he had integrity and character and compassion and honor—all the qualities that really mattered, but which were so lacking in her first husband. Those were the qualities that had made her fall in love with him.

Best of all, he loved her, too. He'd told her so. But he'd also made it clear that he was scared. And that he'd never planned to marry again. He'd been very up front about that. But she sensed that, like her, he'd undergone a change of heart in recent weeks.

Because more and more, she had come to believe that having Mitch in her life—in *their* lives—was in both Bruce's and her best interests. Mitch had graciously offered her time to think things through, but she didn't need any more time to make up her mind. She wanted him in her life. For always. And maybe it was time to tell him that.

Tess took a deep breath and opened her mouth to speak, only to be interrupted by the waiter.

"Could I offer you two some coffee or dessert?"

It took Tess a moment to switch gears, and Mitch seemed to be having the same problem. At last they reluctantly broke eye contact and looked up at the waiter.

"Coffee for both of us," Mitch said, then transferred his gaze to Tess. "How about dessert?" He winked at her wickedly. "I will if you will."

She smiled and reached for her purse, glad now for the interruption. She needed to escape for a moment, compose her thoughts, decide exactly what she wanted to say to Mitch so she didn't sound pushy, just receptive. "Anything chocolate will be fine. Surprise me," she said as she stood. "Will you excuse me for a moment?"

Mitch stood as well, and the warmth in his smile made her tingle. "Hurry back."

He watched her disappear before he took his seat again and turned back to the waiter. "You heard the lady. Bring us two of your best chocolate desserts."

The waiter bowed slightly. "Of course."

Mitch reached for his wineglass and leaned back, willing his pulse to slow down. In a few minutes he was going to ask Tess to be his wife. And he wasn't at all sure of her answer. Yes, they'd acknowledged their love. But they'd also acknowledged their reservations. He'd admitted his fear. What he hadn't yet told her was that now he was more afraid of living without her than of taking another chance on love. On her side, she'd told him of her concerns about Bruce, and he'd promised to give it a little time and see how things worked out. Maybe he was rushing it. But frankly, his patience was wearing thin. He wanted her with him every day, wanted to wake up beside her in the morning and hold her in his arms through the night. He wanted their lives to merge. He wanted to create a new, shared life together. And he didn't want to wait any longer to tell her that. He reached in again and touched the velvet case. In just a few minutes he would…

His pager began to vibrate, and he automatically reached to his belt and shut it off. He probably should have left it in the car, he realized with a frown. That would have eliminated the possibility of distractions. Since he used the pager only for emergencies, the vibrating warning always signaled a crisis of some kind. Karen had the number, as did the president of the school board. And the police, in case there was an off-hours emergency at the school. So a vibrating pager was *not* a good omen.

Mitch debated for a moment, fighting against the urge to check the message. Tonight was supposed to be about him and Tess, alone, and he resented the intrusion. But it simply wasn't in his nature to ignore an emergency—much as he might want to.

He checked his pager. The message was cryptic, and it was from the police. ''Please call ASAP.''

Mitch felt his stomach clench. He'd never been paged by the police. Something must be very wrong.

''Mitch, what is it?''

He looked over at Tess, who had already taken her seat, and frowned. ''I don't know. The police just paged me.''

Her face grew concerned. ''You'd better call right away.''

''Yeah.'' He hesitated for one more moment, then

laid his napkin on the table and stood. "I'll be right back," he promised. "And I'm sorry about the interruption."

She waved his apology aside. "Emergencies come up. Take your time."

He sent her a grateful look and his eyes grew tender. "Thanks for understanding."

It took Mitch only a moment to locate a phone, and a few seconds after that he was talking to the sergeant on duty, whom he knew.

"Thanks for calling so quickly, Mitch."

"Sure, Jack. What's up?"

"Steve just called in. They've got an OD situation, and they found your name and phone number in the kid's pocket. No other ID. Could be one of your students. We need you to do a positive ID."

Mitch's grip tightened on the phone. "Is he…still alive?"

"No."

He closed his eyes and sucked in his breath, feeling the color drain from his face. "Where is he?"

The sound of papers being rustled came over the wire, and then the sergeant gave Mitch the location— a small, largely unused park in Southfield.

"I can be there in fifteen minutes."

"You don't need to do that, Mitch. Might be easier just to stop by the morgue in an hour or so."

"No. I'll go. Thanks, Jack."

"Sure. I'll let Steve know you're on the way."

The line went dead, and Mitch slowly replaced the receiver. His hands were shaking, and he jammed them into the pockets of his slacks, fists clenched. Dear God, it was like being plunged back into his own nightmare! It wasn't *his* son this time. But it was *someone's* son. And deep in his gut he had a feeling he knew who it was. Very few of his students were likely to carry his phone number. Except Tony Watson, who had come to him on more than one occasion to talk through his problems. Who had thought of Mitch as his friend, as someone he could count on. The knot in his stomach twisted more tightly.

He hadn't even reached the table before Tess was on her feet and reaching for her purse. "What's wrong?" she asked, panic edging her voice. "Is it Bruce?"

He shook his head. "No. But the police think they've found one of my students. He overdosed. My name was in his pocket, and there was no other ID. They need me to come and identify him."

"Oh, dear God!" Tess breathed, her face a mask of shock. "Is he…is he alive?"

Mitch shook his head.

She swallowed, and he could see the sheen of tears in her eyes. "Do you want me to come with you?"

Though he hadn't expected that offer, he was tempted to take it. Maybe it would be easier to face if Tess was beside him. But that was selfish. He couldn't subject her to the scene in the park. He'd been there before, and he knew it would give her nightmares for months. Slowly he shook his head. "You don't need to see this. I'll have the restaurant call you a cab."

She studied his face for a moment, then nodded. "Okay."

He reached out to her then, laced his fingers with hers. "I'm sorry about this, Tess."

Her earnest gaze connected with his. "Don't be. I understand." And then she moved closer and wrapped her arms around him, as if she sensed his need for some concrete sign of reassurance and support. Despite the curious, if discreet, glances of diners at nearby tables, he held her fiercely, letting her love envelop him and insulate him for just a moment from the horror ahead, drawing from her the courage to face what was to come.

"Be careful," she whispered close to his ear.

"I will."

"Call me later?"

"It could be late."

"I'll be up."

"Okay."

Reluctantly he released her and stepped away, hesitating long enough to reach over and touch her face. She covered his hand with hers, and for a moment their hearts touched. Then he turned away.

He looked back once, when he reached the door. Tess was still standing by the table, her beautiful features bathed in the golden glow of candlelight. And suddenly he had the oddest feeling. It was almost as if his time with Tess had been merely a dream, a brief respite from his true reality—a destiny of nightmares and loneliness. And as he stepped out into the night, a frightening sense of foreboding swept over him that the dream was about to come to an end.

It was a scene right out of his nightmare. The harsh glare of spotlights. The static buzz of walkie-talkies. The flashing lights on police cars. Reporters jockeying for position behind the police barricade. It was surrealistic—and all too familiar.

Mitch hesitated on the sidelines until Steve noticed him and came forward.

"Sorry to interrupt your evening, Mitch," the officer said.

Mitch tried to speak, but nothing came out. He cleared his throat and tried again. "No problem."

Steve lifted the police tape and Mitch ducked under. "He's over there." The man pointed to a heavily wooded section of the park, then led the way.

Mitch followed. His legs felt wooden, and he had to concentrate on simply putting one foot in front of the other. Steve held aside the brush as they made their way about ten yards into the woods, to a small clearing where a draped body lay. For a moment Mitch thought he was going to lose his dinner, and he forced himself to take several slow, deep breaths.

"I guess you've been here before, in your police days," the officer said sympathetically.

The man's comment jolted Mitch, until he reminded himself that no one on the force knew about David. The man was simply talking in generic terms. "Yeah."

"You never get used to it, though, do you?"

Mitch's throat tightened. "No."

Steve reached down to lift the drape, and Mitch steeled himself. A moment later, when the boy's face was revealed in the glare of a flashlight, his fears were confirmed.

"Do you know him?" Steve asked.

Mitch nodded jerkily. "Tony Watson. He...he was one of my students."

The man gently lowered the shroud and stood, taking down the information Mitch provided on the boy's parents. Then he closed his notebook and gazed down at the draped form, shaking his head. "What a waste." Steve sighed and turned back to Mitch, holding out his hand. "Listen, thanks for coming over. Sorry to interrupt your plans for the evening."

As Mitch made his way back to his car, Steve's words echoed ominously in his mind. For in his gut he had the disquieting premonition that the man had interrupted not only his plans for the evening, but his plans for his life.

Why hadn't Tony called?

The question echoed in Mitch's mind as he drove home. He'd tried so hard to get through to the boy, to let him know that he had a friend, anytime, day or night.

Why hadn't he called?

Mitch went over and over the situation in his mind as he drove. Where had he failed? He'd talked to the boy's parents, though their lack of interest had been evident. He'd set up counseling for Tony, but the boy had gone to only one session. He'd tried to get Tony involved in any number of school activities, introduce him to new people, but always the boy returned to the gang. What else could he have done? he asked himself helplessly.

Mitch pulled into his driveway and for a long moment simply sat behind the wheel, too weary to move. Right about now he had hoped to be planning a future with the woman he loved. Instead, a boy was dead, with no future to look forward to. And somehow he felt at fault. There was something he was missing, some connection he wasn't making, that would point the finger of guilt at him. He knew that instinctively, and his instincts had rarely failed him.

With a tired sigh Mitch eased himself out of the car and let himself into the silent, dark house. The message light was blinking on the phone as he passed, and he remembered his promise to call Tess. It was getting late, but she was probably still…

He stopped abruptly, and suddenly the missing connection fell into place. Tony had had Mitch's phone number in his pocket. Which meant he hadn't forgotten about Mitch's offer of help. But Mitch had left the office without checking his voice mail. Nor had he checked his home voice mail since early this afternoon.

A sick feeling of dread enveloped him as he stared at the blinking light on his answering machine. He didn't want to play back his voice mail—here or at work. But he couldn't hide from the truth. With his heart hammering in his chest, he reached for the phone and forced himself to dial his voice mail at work.

The first few messages were innocuous. The sixth one was like a punch in the gut.

"Mr. Jackson, this is Tony. Tony Watson. Listen, things are kind of…kind of rough right now, you know? I just wanted to talk to somebody, and you said to call anytime so…well, I'm calling. I need to do something to feel better soon, you know? Listen, I'll, uh, I'll try your home number. Yeah. Thanks."

The time on the message was a little after five.

Mitch felt as if his lungs were in a vise, as if the

air was being squeezed out of them. Tony *had* tried to call him. He *had* reached out. Except Mitch hadn't been there.

A muscle in his jaw clenched, and he punched the button on his home machine, which showed two messages. Both were from Tony, and had clearly been made from a cell phone.

"Hey, Mr. Jackson, if you're there maybe you could pick up? It's me, Tony Watson…" There was a pause, and Mitch heard the desperate note in his voice. "Okay, I guess not. Look, life's pretty bad, you know? My mom's gone to Europe or someplace for work, and Dad's pretty out of it on the booze. He's not real nice when he's drunk, so I've been trying to stay out of his way. Only, there's nowhere to go. And school stinks, too. All the kids are creeps—except the guys. I know you don't like me to hang around with them, but a guy's gotta have somebody, you know? And they gave me some stuff to try…. They said it would help me feel better. I don't know, though…"

The line went dead. Mitch steeled himself and punched the button for the last message, his heart hammering painfully.

"It's Tony. Hey, listen, forget those other messages, okay? I feel real good now." He erupted into a peal of high-pitched laughter. "Yeah, I'm okay. Man, this stuff is cool! The guys were right. See ya later."

The line went dead.

Mitch closed his eyes, and his fingers clenched around the receiver. If only he'd played his answering machine back earlier! He might have gotten to Tony in time to dissuade him from using whatever stuff his "friends" had given him. He replaced the phone in the holder, his chest tight with emotion. Once again he had failed to recognize when someone needed him desperately. Just as he'd failed David.

And suddenly he realized that he'd been fooling himself all along. Six years ago he'd learned a very painful lesson—that he was apt to get so caught up in his job that his personal life, and those he loved, suffered. Today the reverse had been demonstrated. He'd put his personal life first, and a boy had died. The message was obvious—he simply couldn't manage both.

He thought of what Uncle Ray had said. That he wasn't the same man he'd been six years ago. Maybe that was true in some ways. But one thing hadn't changed, as he'd tragically learned tonight. He still wasn't able to discern an urgent need for help. He'd missed it with Tony, just as he'd missed it with his own son. And how could someone so out of touch with those who needed him most possibly be a good husband or father?

The sudden ringing of the phone startled him, and he reached for it automatically. "Hello."

"Mitch? It's Tess. I know you said you'd call, but I've been so worried…did you just get in?"

He propped one shoulder against the wall and wearily wiped a hand down his face. "Yeah. A few minutes ago. I was just going to call you."

"Was it…one of your students?"

"Yes. Tony Watson."

Tess frowned. The name sounded familiar. "The boy who was having problems at home? From Bruce's class?"

"That's right."

"Oh, Mitch! What happened?"

He couldn't tell her about the phone calls. Not yet. The pain was too raw. "He couldn't handle life. He thought drugs could help. The classic story."

There was silence for a moment, and he knew that she was thinking how close Bruce had come to going down this same path. "I'm so sorry," she finally said softly.

"Me, too."

"You sound exhausted."

"Yeah."

"Do you want me to come over?"

He closed his eyes and sucked in a breath. Oh, yes! He needed Tess now, desperately. Needed to feel her arms around him, to touch her softness, to inhale her goodness. He needed to hold her until the nightmares receded and he recaptured the dream of their future together. But that could never be. It wouldn't be fair to her. Because he would fail her. Maybe not next week. Or next year. But someday. And he couldn't do that again to someone he loved.

"No. It's late. We both need to get some sleep."

There was a moment's hesitation before she spoke. "All right. We'll talk tomorrow."

"Right."

Again she hesitated. He knew she wanted him to say more. But he couldn't.

"Good night, then."

"Good night," he replied.

He replaced the receiver, then reached into his jacket pocket and removed the velvet box, cradling it gently in his hand. His time with Tess had been a lovely interlude, giving him a tantalizing taste of joy.

Making him believe once again in the magic of love and happily-ever-afters. In the end, though, it had been but a burst of sweetness that quickly dissolved, like cotton candy on the tongue. Though difficult at the time and made only after heartfelt prayers for guidance, his decision six years before appeared to have been the right one after all. He wasn't husband or father material. He'd failed his first wife. He'd failed his son. And now he'd failed Tony.

As a cop, he'd dealt with evidence every day. Sometimes it was difficult to reach a conclusion. But there was no question at all in this instance.

It was an open-and-shut case.

# *Chapter Fourteen*

"I sure don't understand grown-ups, Uncle Ray."

The older man studied the chessboard for a moment before replying. "Why is that?"

"They do stuff that doesn't make sense."

Uncle Ray picked up a knight and made his move. "Anything in particular?"

"Well, like Mr. Jackson. He quit calling Mom. I mean, he was hanging around all the time, then all of a sudden he just disappeared. Mom's been moping around ever since, jumping every time the phone rings like she's hoping it's him. I told her she should call him, but she just got this real sad look and didn't say anything."

Uncle Ray nodded understandingly. "It's hard to lose someone you love, Bruce."

The teenager looked at him in surprise. "How did you know she loved him?"

Uncle Ray tilted his head and his lips turned up in a melancholy smile. "I was in love once. I recognize the signs. And I'll tell you something else. Mitch loves her, too."

Bruce frowned in confusion. "Then why doesn't he call?"

The older man sighed and leaned back in his chair. "Life can be pretty complicated when you're grown up, Bruce. People do things for lots of reasons. Some of them wrong, even when the intentions are good."

Bruce's frown deepened. "Mom said Mr. Jackson stopped coming around because he feels responsible for Tony's death. But what did that have to do with us?"

Uncle Ray regarded the teenager for a moment. "Did Mitch ever tell you about his son?"

Bruce hesitated. "He told me he still misses him."

"Did he tell you what happened to him?"

Bruce looked down and fiddled with a chess piece. "Not exactly. But I…I know."

Now it was Uncle Ray's turn to frown. "How?"

"When we stayed here one night, I heard a noise in the den. By the time I got there, Mom was talking to Mr. Jackson. I think he'd been having a nightmare or something, and Mom heard him, too. Anyway, he told her about his son, and the drugs, and how he…how he found him in that warehouse. I felt real bad for him."

Uncle Ray nodded. "We all did. But no one felt worse than Mitch. He believed he'd failed his son. And the fact is, he had. But he was grieving, too, because his wife had just died. So he wasn't entirely to blame, even though he felt he was. For a long time after that I wasn't sure he was going to make it. But when he did, he decided to spend the rest of his life helping other kids get their act together.''

"Kids like me?''

"Yes. And like Tony. But his plans didn't quite work out, because he met your mom and fell in love.''

"Was that bad?''

"Not at all. I personally think it was the best thing that could have happened. But I'm sure he feels that if he hadn't been with your mom the night Tony died, if he'd picked up his messages, maybe he could have saved him.''

Bruce propped his chin in his hand, his face grave. "Man. That's heavy.''

"Yes, it is. And Mitch might be right. But he'll never be able to save the whole world, no matter how hard he tries. All he can do is his best. And that's plenty good enough, if you ask me. He's done a lot of fine work in the past six years.''

Bruce grinned. "Yeah. Look at me.''

Uncle Ray chuckled. "Good point.''

Once more Bruce's face grew serious. "So he thinks that Mom and I would get in the way of him doing his job.''

"Partly,'' Uncle Ray conceded. "But I think he's even more afraid that his job will get in the way of him being a good husband and father. That eventually he would let you and your mom down.''

Bruce frowned. "He'd never do that. He always tries his best to do what's right. And you can't let somebody down if you're trying your best.''

Uncle Ray leaned forward and once more examined the chessboard. "That's true, son. Trouble is,

I'm not sure how we can convince Mitch that his best would be good enough.''

"There's someone here to see you, Mitch."

Mitch looked at Karen distractedly, then glanced at his watch. "Why are you still here?"

"I was keeping your visitor company."

Mitch frowned and transferred his gaze to his calendar. "I don't have anything scheduled."

"He doesn't have an appointment."

"Who is it?"

"Bruce Lockwood. He's been waiting for three hours."

Mitch felt his heart stop, then race on. He was on his feet instantly. "Three hours! What's wrong?"

"Nothing that I can determine," Karen said calmly. "Relax. He said it wasn't an emergency. I asked that first thing. But he insisted on waiting, even though I told him you were busy all afternoon. I tried to break in and let you know he was here, but you went right from the committee meeting to three conference calls back-to-back and I couldn't get a word in edgewise. Which is a record for me. I suggested he try another day, when you weren't so busy, but he refused to leave."

Mitch frowned. "Then it must be important." He flexed the muscles in his shoulders and sighed wearily. "Send him in, okay?"

She tilted her head and regarded him disapprovingly. "I thought these long days were over. I think you're regressing."

Instead of responding, he nodded toward the door. "Go home, Dr. Freud. And send in Bruce." She gave him an exasperated look and started to leave, but paused when he spoke again. "Thanks for waiting, Karen. And for caring."

She looked back and smiled. "No problem."

By the time Bruce entered a moment later, looking slightly ill at ease, Mitch had moved out from behind his desk. "Hello, Bruce. Come in. I'm sorry you waited so long. I had no idea you were out there."

"It's okay. I know you're busy."

"Not that busy. Sit down." He motioned toward the chairs off to the side. "Does your mom know where you are?"

"Yeah. I said I had a meeting after school. She's gonna pick me up when I'm finished," the boy replied, perching tensely on the edge of a chair.

"So what can I do for you?" Mitch asked, trying hard to maintain simple professional friendliness when what he really wanted to do was put his arm around the boy's hunched shoulders.

Bruce fidgeted and broke eye contact. "Since it's the last week of school I guess I won't see you for a while, so I just wanted to stop in and see...see how you were. I guess I got used to you being around the apartment, and it's kind of weird now that it's just Mom and me."

Mitch's gut clenched, and he took a deep breath. The boy hadn't come right out and said he missed Mitch, but the implication was clear. Mitch tried to swallow past the lump that suddenly appeared in his throat. "I'm fine," he lied, striving for a conversational tone. "How about you and your mom?"

Bruce shrugged. "We're okay, I guess. But Mom...well...she misses you. A lot."

The knot in Mitch's stomach tightened, and the sudden pressure in his chest squeezed the air out of his lungs. "I miss her, too," he said, his voice not quite steady. "And you."

Bruce studied him, as if trying to discern his sincerity. "Yeah?"

"Yeah."

There was silence for a moment before Bruce spoke again. "I've been thinking about Tony a lot."

A spasm of pain tightened Mitch's features. "I have, too."

"He was an okay kid, you know? He just didn't have much of a life. Things were pretty bad at home."

"I know. He told me about some of it."

"Yeah, he said he talked to you once in a while. He said you helped him a lot."

Another twist of the knife. "Not enough, though."

Bruce gazed at him steadily. "You did your best, Mr. Jackson. Tony told me that you were the only one who ever really cared about him. His own mom and dad only cared about their own stuff. She was gone all the time, and his dad always criticized him, telling him he would never amount to anything." Bruce paused and took a deep breath, his own voice suddenly none too steady. "That's real tough, you know? My dad was like that, too. Nothing I ever did was good enough for him. But at least I had my mom. I knew she loved me no matter what, and that made a really big difference. But Tony didn't have that. He didn't have anyone who cared about him, except you."

Bruce leaned closer, his voice urgent—and earnest.

"He told me once that he wished he'd had a dad like you. That maybe things would have been different. But see, you weren't his dad, Mr. Jackson. You couldn't do all the things a dad is supposed to do. Tony needed a real, full-time dad. And a mom. They were the ones who let him down, not you."

Bruce stood then, and a flush slowly crept up his neck. "I gotta get home, but…but there's something else I wanted to say." He hesitated, and the flush moved to his face. "I just wanted you to know that I think Tony was right about one thing. You really would make a great dad."

Mitch felt the sudden sting of tears behind his eyes, and his throat constricted with emotion. For months the boy had considered him an enemy. But somewhere along the way he'd earned Bruce's respect and affection—to the point that the boy would welcome him as a father. It was the most flattering, most moving thing anyone had ever said to him.

Except, that is, when Tess had said, "I love you." Even after he'd revealed his greatest flaws, when he'd told her about his failures as a husband and father, she had still found it in her heart to love him. Surely there could be no greater compliment—or miracle—than that. She believed that his past failures, rather than diminishing him, had forged his character. Like Uncle Ray, she believed that he had changed over the past six years. And as Bruce had pointed out, with insight beyond his years, Mitch *had* done his best with Tony. It was just that he simply couldn't be the father Tony—and so many other boys—desperately needed. There just wasn't enough of him to go around. And that would be true whether he had his own family or remained single, he realized.

Suddenly he recalled Uncle Ray's words when the older man had talked about selling the farm. *Time brings changes,* he'd said. *People change. Circumstances change. And sometimes you just have to realize that it's time to move on.*

Bruce shifted uncomfortably and jammed his hands into his pockets as the silence lengthened. "Anyway, that's what I wanted to tell you," he said self-consciously, transferring his gaze to the toe of his shoe.

Slowly Mitch rose and reached over to put his arm around the boy's tense shoulders. "Thank you, Bruce," he said huskily. "I wasn't the best father before, so it's nice to know someone thinks I'm up to the job now." He drew a deep breath, and in that moment made a decision that he knew would affect the rest of his life. "How about I give you a ride home?"

Bruce stared at him, his face guarded but hopeful. "You don't have to do that."

"I want to," he said gently. "You and I have done a lot of fence-mending with Uncle Ray lately. Maybe it's time for me to mend another kind of fence with your mom. What do you think?"

The caution in Bruce's eyes gave way to joy, and he grinned broadly at Mitch. "Awesome!"

Tess heard the front door open, and with a frown she tossed the dish towel on the counter and headed for the living room. "Bruce, is that you? I thought you were going to…'' Her voice died as she stepped across the threshold.

''Hi, Mom. Mr. Jackson gave me a ride home.''

With an effort, Tess transferred her gaze from Mitch's intense eyes to her son. She drew a deep breath, struggling to cope with this unexpected turn of events. ''Y-your dinner's in the oven,'' she said distractedly.

''Cool. See you guys later.''

With that he breezed by, pausing only to bestow a quick kiss on Tess's forehead. She stared after him, thrown off balance by his uncharacteristically affectionate behavior, which had largely disappeared with the onset of adolescence.

''Can I interest you in a cup of coffee?''

Tess's gaze swiveled back to Mitch. He looked as if he'd been through hell in the two weeks since she'd seen him. His face was haggard, and there were dark circles under his eyes, as if he hadn't slept in days. Her heart overflowed with love for this extraordinary man, who cared so deeply about others that he took on their burdens as if they were his own. She wanted to go to him, pull him close and hold him fiercely to her heart until he understood that their love wasn't a liability to his work, but an asset. Just as his work was an asset to their love, for it was what had made him the man he was today—compassionate, caring, committed. She wanted to hold him until he believed what Uncle Ray had said, that he *was* a different man from the one who'd lost his son six years before. That the incident with Tony, while tragic, didn't mean he had failed. It just meant he was human. That he could have missed Tony's call for any number of reasons, not necessarily personal ones. That he was the man who had earned her eternal gratitude for saving her son. That he was the man she loved with all her heart and wanted to spend the rest of her life with.

Tess wanted to say all those things. But her voice had deserted her. All she could do was stare at Mitch, as if trying to reassure herself that he wasn't a mirage.

Meanwhile, Mitch took his own inventory. The fine lines at the corners of Tess's eyes were new, and her face seemed taut and strained. Clearly, his unexpected arrival had only added to her distress. Her shallow breathing was reflected in the rapid rise and fall of her chest, and her hand was white-knuckled on the door frame. Above the V of her soft sweater he could see the wild beating of her pulse, and her hand was trembling when she raised it to her throat.

A surge of remorse swept over Mitch, leaving a bitter taste in his mouth. Tess had offered him her love, and he'd pulled back for reasons he'd felt at the time were noble and selfless, putting her through hell in the process. But he'd been wrong, and he intended to do everything in his power to make amends.

"Coffee w-would be nice," Tess said breathlessly when she finally found her voice. "I'll just let Bruce know and—"

"I'll be fine, Mom," her son called out, clearly tuned in to the conversation in the living room. "Take your time."

She flushed, and Mitch gave her a crooked grin. "So much for privacy," she muttered as she walked past him toward the door.

He followed her out, then nodded toward a bench tucked beneath a flowering crab apple tree in a tiny park across the street. "I'm not retracting my offer of coffee, but do you mind if we just sit for a few minutes first? I have a few things I'd like to say privately."

Tess nodded, gathering her courage. "So do I."

He held out his hand, in a gesture of…friendship? Apology? Empathy? She had no idea, but she would happily accept any of the three. Because his reaching out told her more eloquently than words that he still cared, that the dialogue was still open. And that gave her new hope that maybe, just maybe, he'd had a change of heart. She looked down at his long, lean fingers, then slipped her hand into his, closing her eyes for a moment to savor the feel of his strong yet gentle touch.

When their gazes reconnected, she read much in his—gratitude, repentance, tenderness…and yes, love. It was what she had dreamed of seeing every night for the past two weeks, when she had at last managed to fall into a restless sleep. But now she began to hope that maybe, just maybe, her dream might really come true.

He gave her fingers a gentle squeeze, and the warmth in his eyes was like the caress of the sun on a spring day, holding the promise of new life after a long, dark winter. There was a sense of unreality about the scene, an almost too-good-to-be-true quality, but their linked hands dispelled any notion of make-believe. Mitch was here, every wonderful, handsome inch of him, and Tess knew with absolute certainty that this was where they belonged—together, for always. She prayed that Mitch had reached the same conclusion. But if he hadn't, she was prepared to fight for what she knew was their destiny.

Mitch led her to the bench, angling his body toward hers as they sat, never relinquishing his hold on her hand. "First of all, as inadequate as the words are, I want you to know how sorry I am for what I put you through these past two weeks," he said huskily. "And all because of some misguided notion that I could be all things to all people. But the fact is, I realize I can't be a father to every boy who needs one. I can be a support system, I can help, but I can't take the place of a father and a mother, of parents who are in their life every day and every night. To think otherwise is not only unrealistic, it's arrogant."

Impulsively Tess reached over and laid her hand tenderly on his cheek. He immediately covered it with his own as their gazes locked. "Not arrogant, Mitch. Never arrogant," she said fervently. "Your only fault, if it can even be called that, is that you care *too* much. You want to help everyone who is in pain. And you go out of your way to avoid inflicting pain on others. You may not always succeed, but you do a far better job of it than most people. You don't need to apologize for doing what you think is right."

The deep, unconditional love in Tess's clear green eyes told Mitch all he needed to know. She still loved him. And she was willing to give him another chance to prove he loved her.

This time Mitch didn't hesitate. He pulled her into his arms, buried his face in her soft hair, and in her loving embrace found solace for the anguish and regret in his heart, forgiveness for the pain he'd inflicted on her. He held her tightly, his hands on her back, in her hair, pressing her close, as if he never wanted to let her go.

"I love you, Tess," he whispered fiercely, his voice ragged with emotion. "You've brought sunshine back to my soul, filled my days with a joy I never hoped to find again, given me hope for a brighter tomorrow than I ever dared dream of. I can't promise you a perfect life, but I can promise that I'll try my best to be the kind of husband and father you and Bruce deserve."

He pulled back and looked down at her shimmering eyes, and his own face softened with love as he traced the path of one tear down her cheek with a gentle finger. "I never wanted to make you cry, Tess," he said softly. "That's what held me back—I was so afraid I would end up hurting you and Bruce."

"*I'm* not afraid, Mitch. Because I love you, and I know that together we can make this work."

The absolute trust in her eyes and the conviction in her voice made his throat tighten with emotion, and he shook his head wonderingly. "What did I ever do to deserve you?" he said in awe, cupping her face with his hands.

"I've been asking myself that same question. I never thought I'd find a man like you."

"Believe me, I'm getting the better end of this deal, Tess. I'm far from perfect."

"You're perfect for me."

He shook his head and gave her a crooked smile. "You have all the right answers."

She shook her head firmly. "No. I've had a lot of wrong answers. And made a lot of bad decisions. But I'm willing to trust my heart on this one."

"So am I. It just took me longer to realize something you seemed to know all along…that love doesn't *get* in the way—it *lights* the way."

The smile she gave him was luminous. "What a beautiful thought."

"No more beautiful than you." Then he took her hands in his, and with his gaze locked on hers, spoke in a voice that was steady and sure. "I planned to ask you this question two weeks ago. I'd like to try again now. Tess Lockwood, would you do me the great honor of becoming my wife?"

Tess's eyes once more brimmed with tears. "Yes," she breathed, her own voice choked with emotion. "Oh, yes!"

Mitch's heart soared with joy. He framed her face with his hands, giving himself one brief moment to glory in her radiance before he lowered his lips to hers in a kiss that was gratitude, hunger, passion and tenderness all in one. As his lips moved over hers, at times giving, at times demanding, she met him every step of the way. It was a kiss filled with need, with hope and with the urgency of long-restrained passion suddenly released. Mitch tangled his fingers in her soft hair, cupping her head as his other hand splayed across her back, molding her body even closer to his. He felt her trembling, but he also felt her sweet surrender to fate…destiny…divine Providence…whatever force had brought them together. And with her in his arms, he had the courage to surrender as well, to recognize that the gift of Tess's love had at last freed him from the legacy of loneliness that had shadowed his life for the past six years. As he held her close, he knew that this woman was, above all things, a miracle, for she had given him back his life. And he sent a silent, heartfelt prayer of thanks heavenward.

Tess felt as if she was drowning in a sea of emotion, overwhelmed by a joy like none she had ever before experienced and by a passion intensified and enriched by the promise of a lifelong commitment. Here, in this man's strong, sure arms, she felt loved and cherished and protected. If for years she had considered herself more mom than romantic interest, tonight she felt all woman. Mitch had awakened in her a hunger that had long lain dormant, had brought to life a passion that she thought had long ago been extinguished. And his kiss tonight, which sealed their engagement, held the promise of so much more, filling her with excitement, eagerness—and gratitude to the Lord for sending this very special man into her life and for giving her the courage to take another chance on love.

When Mitch at last reluctantly eased away, his lips warm and lingering, Tess felt as if every nerve in her body was vibrating. And when their gazes connected, she was able to utter but one simple word.

"Wow!"

He grinned crookedly and leaned over to nuzzle her neck. "My sentiments exactly," he agreed, his warm lips leaving a trail of fire against her skin. "I hope you aren't planning on a long engagement."

"H-how does a couple of weeks sound?" she said faintly.

He groaned. "Too long." His lips claimed hers once again in a lingering, spell-weaving kiss that sent her world spinning out of orbit.

At last, with great reluctance, she pulled back. "We'll never make it two weeks if we keep this up," she said with a shaky grin. "And we need to set a good example for Bruce."

Mitch's gaze momentarily flickered to the apartment behind Tess, and suddenly his mouth twitched in amusement. "Speaking of Bruce…I think he just got a great preview of romance 101."

Her eyes widened and her cheeks grew red. "Tell me he isn't watching."

Mitch grinned. "I can't do that without lying."

Tess frowned and bit her lip. "I wanted to sort of prepare him. I mean, I'm not sure he's ready for us to get married."

Mitch chuckled. "Oh, he's ready, all right."

Tess looked at him, puzzled. "How do you know?"

"Because he came to see me this afternoon. Waited three hours, in fact. He was a man with a mission. And then he gave it to me straight, laid it on the line about Tony. He also told me that he thought I'd make a great father." Mitch's voice caught on the last word.

Tess stared at him. "He said all that?"

"Mmm-hmm. And he was very happy when I told him I was going to talk to you tonight. So I think you can be sure that he'll be pleased at the outcome."

Tess shifted her position so she, too, could see the window of the apartment. Sure enough, Bruce was standing there, a huge grin plastered on his face. Mitch raised his hand, and Bruce gave them a very clear thumbs-up sign.

"See what I mean?" Mitch said with a smile.

Tess turned back to him, and once more her eyes

glistened with unshed tears. "I think this is what they call a happy ending."

"I think it is," he replied with a grin. "So what do you say the three of us go out and celebrate?"

A euphoric joy radiated through Tess, filling her with absolute happiness and contentment, and she smiled radiantly. "I think that would be awesome!"

\*   \*   \*   \*   \*

Dear Reader,

As I write this letter, the school year is ending— and I find myself envying the students who have a carefree summer ahead, with no worries over tasks yet to be completed or issues to be resolved. For someone who has spent many years in the corporate world, that kind of closure seems very, very appealing. As does the opportunity to make a fresh beginning each fall.

Life is filled with such endings and beginnings, many of them externally imposed and out of our control. Like moving from one grade to the next. But sometimes we have to take the initiative and recognize that it's up to us to make the decision to move on.

In *Crossroads,* Mitch and Tess face that challenge. So do Bruce and Uncle Ray. Though their challenges differ, they must each choose to end one way of life before they can start another.

Such choices are not usually easy. They require us to take a long, hard look at our priorities, our fears and hopes. They also require trust—in ourselves, in others and in God. As you face such turning points in your life, may you take comfort in knowing that you are never alone. For as the Lord promised, "I am with you always, even to the end of time."

Irene Hannon

# Love Inspired®

## HEART OF STONE

### BY

## LENORA WORTH

Stone Dempsey had struggled with his faith, but
found a kindred spirit and a reason to believe
again. Because shy Tara Parnell, a struggling
widow with a stubborn streak, entered his world.
Would this rugged businessman make the deal of
his lifetime—for a bride?

### Don't miss

## HEART OF STONE

### On sale November 2003

*Available at your favorite retail outlet.*

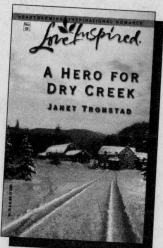